October Nights

Also by James B. Christensen

Honeymoon Phase

The Vessel

October Nights

James B. Christensen

ISBN-13: 978-0692962732 (Ravensbook Media)
ISBN-10: 0692962735

For Laura and Abby

CONTENTS

The Cradle

Darkness fled as the overhead lights flickered on, separating what had come before from what came next. The fluorescent bulbs hummed and looked down on a sterile laboratory like any of the thousands that dotted the world—countertops and sinks, beakers, and test tubes. Cupboards, desks, and computers.

Along one white-painted brick wall sat five large capsules meant for human hibernation. A woman lay in each one. All of them asleep. Tubes, pipes, and wires led to each capsule. Computer monitors displayed a dizzying array of readouts. On the wall above each capsule was a sign bearing a name in quotes. From left to right they were: "Diana," "Sara," "Lucy," "Ann," and "Jill."

Four of the capsule lids were open, releasing clouds of steam as the warm, humid air from within mixed with the cooler air of the room. Diana's capsule remained shut. It was the rising lids from these units that triggered the motion-sensitive lights.

In the capsule at the right end, Jill's eyes fluttered open and glanced around, squinting at the bright lights reflecting off omnipresent white. She frowned in confusion and sat up, her muscles tight and sore from a nap whose length she could only guess. She scanned the setting and its trappings. Nothing jogged her memory. She glanced at the row of capsules to her right, noting the closed unit on the end, and the three naked women resting in the other units.

Jill glanced down at her own unclothed body and gasped at the symbols drawn on her skin. Straight, scarlet lines with curvy squiggles sprouting from them. Electrodes stuck to her arms, chest, face, and thighs. She tried to gather her thoughts, but her mind was empty of everything but questions: Who am I? Why am I here? On and on they went, with no answers.

She drew her knees up to her chest, trying to fold in on herself and hide, vulnerable in her nakedness yet claustrophobic in the capsule. If she wanted answers, she had to get up and walk around, bare or not. She peeled off the electrodes, tossed them and their attached wires aside, stepped out of the capsule, and stood. The cold, lime linoleum chilled her toes, and she shivered. A few unsteady steps brought back her leg strength. She tentatively walked around the lab, arms crossed over her breasts, looking for anyone who might work there, feeling like she'd accidentally locked herself out of the shower.

The rising steam from the other capsules had dissipated enough for Jill to see symbols on their sleeping bodies, too. The lab was empty except for them. To the left of the capsules was a door secured via keypad lock. A rectangle of glass in the door opened into the darkness of that room.

The side wall, perpendicular to the capsule wall, had a sliding glass door, also with a keypad, and likewise looked into a dark room. Light spillage revealed the outer contours of another lab, with a table or platform in the center. Opposite that wall, on the far end of the lab, was a small workstation and a security desk.

Jill walked to the security desk where, on the wall opposite the capsules, was another sliding glass door. A hallway stretched into the blackness. There was no keypad, no visible way to open the door. Jill waved her arms to activate any motion sensor that might be present. The door didn't move.

Jill's breathing quickened and tears of fear and frustration tickled her eyelids. She studied her reflection in the glass and got a better look at the writing on her body. The symbols were arranged in an obvious, but unknown, pattern. They swirled up and down her body, even decorating her toes. She gave her backside to the reflection. Symbols covered her back, buttocks, and legs. Looking at her front again, the angle and flow of the writing appeared to focus attention on her breasts, abdomen, and pubic area. She struggled to remember how this had happened, how she came to be covered in markings and sleeping in a capsule here, wherever "here" was.

Tears spilled down her cheek. She rubbed at the writing, first lightly then hard, panicked rubbing, but it would not come off nor smudge. She wanted to scream, but didn't want to wake her companions, whoever they were. To be honest, she was afraid to scream and discover they were alone, or to scream and not like who came running. She stood alone and waited for an idea.

"Where are we?"

Jill yelped in surprise and spun to find Lucy sitting up in her capsule, looking around. Sara and Ann stirred in their capsules. Lucy noted Jill's naked body and the symbols on her skin then looked at her own.

"What is all of this?" Lucy asked.

Jill retreated behind the security desk to hide her lower body. She covered her chest. Lucy freed herself from her electrodes and stood. She wavered for two seconds until her equilibrium adjusted. Seeing Jill's efforts to cover up, she also crossed her arms.

Ann and Sara sat up, groggy and bewildered.

Lucy walked to the sliding glass door leading to the outer hallway. She kept her body out of sight and pounded on the door.

"Hello!"

The others winced at the sound.

"The doors won't open," Jill said. "They're all locked."

Lucy looked at the room. She looked up at the ceiling. Sniffed the air. Listened.

"It's windy," she said.

Jill cocked her head and listened. "I don't hear anything."

Sara and Ann watched the other two, confused.

"Where are we?" Ann asked, having to clear her throat to speak.

"I don't know," Jill said.

"Oh my God!" Sara said, seeing the symbols on her naked body.

Ann noticed her own marked body and put her arm across her breasts.

Lucy stared at Jill. "Who are you?"

Jill pointed at her capsule. "According to that, I'm Jill."

Everyone looked at the name plates.

"Why are our names in quotes?" Ann asked.

"Because they aren't our real names," Lucy said. "Just a guess."

"Does anyone remember their name?" Jill asked.

No   one   remembered.

"Anything? About yourselves or this place?" Lucy asked.

More silence.

"It looks like we're patients," Ann said.

"So where are the doctors?" Sara asked.

"I—"

"—don't know," Lucy said. "Let's assume all questions are rhetorical from now on."

"How does everyone feel?" Ann asked. "If we're being treated for something, maybe we have symptoms."

Other than dizziness and slight nausea, everyone felt well and reported increasing strength as the sleep effects wore off.

"What is this?" Sara asked, gesturing frantically at the writing on her body. "I don't remember *anything*."

She cried and hugged herself, rocking back and forth. Lucy went to her and took the girl's face in her hands and spoke softly. "We don't know. Okay? None of us do."

Sara grew more hysterical.

"Shhh! This won't help."

Sara calmed.

"We need answers. Can you help us?"

Sara nodded. "I want to know what this stuff on my body is."

"That's as good a place to start as any," Lucy said.

She stood and let her arms drop to her sides. "Ladies, we're gonna have to lose our shyness."

"Nothing we haven't seen before, I guess," Ann said.

"As far as you know," Jill said.

"Either way, we're wearing birthday suits for now, and that's how it is," Lucy said.

The others gradually lowered their arms, too.

"Let's compare these symbols," Lucy said. "Come on, you girls get up."

Lucy helped Sara stand. Jill came around the desk to help Ann. The women gathered in an open space near the security desk and looked at each other's bodies. Shy at first, but taking a closer look as they tried to decode the lines and waves. They turned around and scanned their backs.

"Looks like the same symbols. Same patterns," Ann said.

"Why do the symbols point to . . ." Sara began.

"The good stuff?" Jill said.

"Is this some sort of sexual thing?" Sara asked.

"Here? Seems inappropriate," Lucy said.

"Or biological," Ann said. "Those parts aren't only for sex. They're for reproduction and nurturing, too."

"I'll bet you're a load of fun in the sack," Jill said.

"I wish I knew."

Jill inspected Ann's body, comparing her to herself and the others. Lucy and Sara were young, fit, and muscular like Jill. Ann, while not overweight, was softer in the arms and thighs and had a slight paunch to her belly. Her breasts were twice as large as theirs. There were small crow's feet at the corner of her eyes. She looked at least ten years older than the other three.

Ann noticed Jill's visual exam.

"What?" Ann asked, her voice sharp.

Jill flinched. "Nothing."

"Why are you staring at me?"

Now Lucy and Sara stared at her. Ann covered herself as best she could and backed away.

"*What is it?*"

"Your symbols are different."

They all looked.

"No, they're not! They're the same!" Ann said.

"I mean they're done differently."

Ann glared at Lucy, then looked at the writing.

"Looks like it was done with a different hand," Sara said.

"Like whoever did yours was in a hurry," Jill said.

Ann studied the markings on her skin. She couldn't deny there was a difference. She looked up at the others and saw suspicion in their eyes.

"I was in one of those things, like you," Ann said. "I am marked up, like you. I am trapped here and suffering amnesia, *just like you.*"No one argued.

"If I'm in on some conspiracy, I'm pretty damn stupid about it!"

"Okay, calm down," Lucy said. "But the fact is that you're different. I don't know what it means, but we need to be on the lookout for what it might mean."

Ann nodded, accepting that. She wiped a tear. "Just remember this is happening to me, too."

"Okay. We will."

"So the symbols are the same," Jill said.

"And mine were done by a different hand," Ann said.

Her fear gave way to an officious manner.

"And I'm older," she said.

The others reacted with surprise.

"Don't act shocked. You can tell," Ann said. "I can see it, too. You all look like a college volleyball team. I look like the coach."

Everyone made the comparison. No one knew what it meant.

"How's everyone feeling now?" Ann asked.

Everyone checked their own condition, stretching, taking deep breaths, wiggling toes, etc.

"Any headaches?"

Nobody had a headache.

"I'm hungry," Sara said.

They had to laugh.

"Me, too," Jill said. "I guess that makes us normal."

Ann and Sara looked around the room, taking in the doors and everything else. Jill and Lucy watched them, waiting to see if they had any new ideas.

"I assume we're locked in?" Ann asked.

"The doors won't open," Lucy said.

Sara rubbed at the writing on her arms.

"It won't come off," Jill said.

"I wonder where we are," Lucy said. "You know, New York City or Los Angeles."

"Or a serial killer's basement," Sara said.

"Oh, shut up!" Jill said.

"I don't hear cars or people or anything that might give away a place," Sara said.

"I hear wind," Lucy said.

"I hear voices," Jill said. "Very faint. Sounds like a radio."

The others listened.

"You hear that?" she asked. "Must be in another room."

"I can't hear it," Ann said.

Nobody else heard a radio. Their anxiety grew in the silence.

"I want to get the hell out of here," Jill said. "We'll attract attention when people see us, that's for sure."

"Maybe we could find something to wrap up in," Ann said. "It's wintertime out there for all we know."

They walked to the far end of the room where the cupboards and desks were.

"I didn't think to check in here for anything," Jill said.

The cupboards were locked.

"High security here," Sara said. "Add that clue to the mystery."

A search of the desk drawers, most of them unlocked, yielded a metal ruler which was strong enough to force the cupboards open. They rummaged through the shelves, finding lab and office supplies.

"Bingo!" Jill said.

She placed a small bin on the security desk. Inside were rows of plastic-wrapped undergarments. The women gushed with relief as they tore open the wrappers. Inside each package was a pair of panties and a tank top, both made of a thin, white fabric. They got dressed.

"See-through and skimpy," Jill said. "I guarantee you a man ordered these. Stupid."

"One size fits nobody," Sara said.

Ann couldn't get the small top over her chest. She sighed in frustration. Lucy unwrapped another set and knotted two tops together to make a makeshift bra for her. As she stapled it together at Ann's shoulder blades, Ann got a worried look on her face.

"What is it?" Sara asked.

"I don't think we're patients," Ann said.

"You can't know that," Lucy said.

"Why not?" Jill asked.

"All of this, leaving us in there naked. These little paper underwears. It all adds up to nobody giving a damn about us or our dignity."

"If we're not patients, what are we?" Sara asked.

". . . Specimens, maybe?" Ann said.

"Knock it off," Lucy said. "You have no idea if that's the case. As far as I'm concerned these clothes feel like a Versace dress compared to how we woke up. We're dressed, now let's get out of here."

"What about her?" Jill asked, pointing to Diana's capsule. "Why didn't hers open up?"

Everyone looked at the sealed unit.

"There's a blinking red light by her head," Sara said. "Everyone else's is green."

"Oh my God," Ann said. Ann ran to Diana's capsule. The others followed.

"What's wrong?" Sara asked.

"Something's happening to her!" Ann said.

Through the glass lid, they saw Diana writhing around, as if waking from a nightmare. Her eyes were wide and her mouth bobbed open like a fish gasping out of water.

"She can't breathe!" Ann said, tugging at the lid.

It didn't budge.

"Help me open it!" Ann said.

All of them dug their fingers under the lip of the lid and pulled. They strained and grunted, but the lid stayed shut. Diana continued to twist and punch the inside of the lid.

"She'll die!" Jill said.

Ann stepped away and paced with her hands pressed against her temples, trying to think of a solution.

"Do something!" Lucy said to Ann.

"Why me?"

"She's getting weak!" Sara said.

Ann rushed to the capsule and reached under the foot end of the unit. She pulled open a small, metal door and reached in. The lid hissed open and rose into the air. Steam swirled out of the chamber as the others helped Diana to her feet. Diana coughed, gasped, and wheezed as air returned to her lungs.

Jill and Sara lowered Diana to the ground when it was clear she couldn't stand.

Lucy walked to Ann, who stared in disbelief at the open hole at the foot of the chamber. Lucy squatted and looked into the hole to see a manual release lever. Ann avoided Lucy's look and stood. Lucy followed. They looked at Diana, watching as she caught her breath.

"How did you know?" Lucy asked Ann.

Jill and Sara looked up to follow the conversation.

"You pulled a *hidden* lever to open the lid," Lucy said. "You knew. *How?*"

"I don't know, dammit," Ann said. "You forget—"

"You're in here just like us," Jill said. "That crap's getting old. You can't ride that forever."

"Suppose your memory comes back?" Sara asked. "Will you tell us then?"

Ann stood under their judgment in silence. "Honestly? I can't say. I don't know what kind of person I am. Or was. Whatever."

"Don't take this personally, but we have to be suspicious of you," Lucy said.

"Fine," Ann said. "I'm suspicious of all of you. Maybe I'm different because I'm the victim. Maybe we all played a part in this, and there are no victims here. Only guilty people. I am *terrified* of my memory coming back."

She pointed to the rest of them.

"So should you."

Everyone was silent, wondering what stories would be revealed when their individual books were opened.

"Are you okay?" Ann asked.

She spoke to Diana. Everyone waited for her to answer. Her eyes looked vaguely at Ann, but were otherwise unfocused.

"Can you hear me?" Ann asked.

Diana responded with a series of childlike coos and babbles. She gestured clumsily with her arms, as if she knew the point she wanted to make, but was unable.

"It's like she's drunk," Sara said. Ann knelt for a close look at Diana, who shrunk away when she leaned in.

"She's scared of you," Jill said.

Ann sighed in exasperation.

"Your insistence on pointing out the obvious is starting to appear desperate."

"Stop it," Sara said. "Let's try to move forward."

"She's right," Lucy said. "Let's find out the truth and let the chips fall where they may."

Ann turned away from her staredown with Jill and examined Diana as best she could.

"Beats me what's wrong," Ann said. "If I had to guess, I'd say she's suffering brain damage from lack of oxygen. Who was out first?"

"I was," Jill said.

"Was her light blinking red the whole time?"

"Beats me," Jill said. "I don't know how these things work."

Jill saw everyone make the *as far as you know* expression and ignored them.

"We'll have to watch out for her," Lucy said.

"Will she go back to normal?" Sara asked.

"Depends on how long she was without oxygen," Ann said. "And no, I have no idea how I know these things."

"Don't get touchy," Lucy said. "But we have to figure out how you know."

"I'm open to ideas," Ann said.

"Okay. You knew how to open the container she was in," Lucy said. "Can you think of any reason you would know that? What was your mindset when you did it?"

"Fear," Ann said. "I wasn't thinking, really, I just . . ."

"Just what?" Jill asked.

Ann started singing to herself. The others looked from her to each other as if Ann's brain had lost oxygen, too.

She belted out her song and walked to the door next to the capsule row. Looking at the ceiling as she sang, she tapped in a numerical code on the keypad. The keypad lit up green, and the door lock clacked open. Jill pushed the door open and grinned at the others.

"How?" Lucy asked.

"I acted without thinking," Ann said.

"Muscle memory," Jill said.

"That's it," Ann said.

"You work here," Sara said.

"Safe to say," Ann said.

"Hot damn, then. Let's muscle memory our way out of here," Lucy said. "Which way out?"

Ann began to sing again and walked in the opposite direction, toward the sliding-glass door that led to the hallway. There, she paused.

"No keypad," she said.

Jill jogged to the security desk. "This has to be a guard post. Must be a button."

She searched around the desk.

"Ah ha!"

She pressed a red button on the desk and grinned. Everyone walked to the door. Sara helped Diana to her feet.

The door didn't move.

Lucy and Jill checked around the desk. Lucy came up with a severed cord.

"Sabotage," she said.

"Cut from the wall," Jill said. "No way to patch it."

"Now what?" Sara asked.

They tried to think of the next step. Diana talked in baby babble again, and the others turned to face her. They gave her the same visual once-over they had given each other.

"Same markings," Jill said. "No surprise there."

"She's older," Ann said. "Older than me, even."

Diana was fit but just this side of unhealthy thinness. Her body was straight, not much curve to it. Streaks of gray ribboned her brown hair.

"In her forties or fifties, I would guess," Sara said. "So she stands out, too," Jill said, looking at Ann.

"I guess she does," Ann said. "Maybe she works here, too."

"We can't leave her alone," Lucy said. "She could hurt herself."

"I'll stay with her," Sara said.

She pulled Diana to her feet and walked her over to the security desk to get her dressed. As she helped Diana step into a pair of panties, Lucy turned to the others.

"I guess we could check out this room," she said, pointing to the open door Ann had unlocked.

When they stepped in, the lights flickered on. To their left was a row of workstations. Empty chairs faced dark computer screens. Personal mementos like photos, plants, and cutesy posters decorated the cubicles. Ann walked along the stations and froze when she came to the end. This one was empty of any personalization.

"What is it?" Lucy asked, seeing Ann's reaction.

"Something about this workspace," Ann said.

"Yours?"

"Might be."

"It's empty," Jill said. "How could it be yours?"

"Maybe I was fired," Ann said.

"Can you log in?" Lucy asked. "Doing your muscle memory trick?"

"I'll try."

Lucy turned to Jill. "Let's look around."

Ann sat at the computer while Lucy and Jill explored the rest of the room. It was roughly the same size as the capsule room. There was a center table. The walls were lined with the usual lab supplies along with strange gadgets and machines of unknown purpose.

"What is this stuff?" Jill asked.

Ann glanced at the room. "I don't know."

"You don't remember, you mean," Jill said. "Or you remember, but won't tell."

Ann glared at her. She looked at Lucy for support, but Lucy didn't come to her defense. Lucy turned away and faced a horizontal device with a lid.

"Looks like a tanning bed," Jill said. "Or a coffin."

"You know what this is?" Lucy called out to Ann.

Ann didn't turn around. "My answers don't satisfy anyone, so stop bothering me."

Lucy and Jill exchanged a glance.

"Keep looking around," Lucy said. "I'm gonna watch over her shoulder."

Jill nodded and resumed her inspection of the room. She spotted a narrow hallway leading from the lab and pointed to it. Lucy acknowledged her plan and went to Ann's desk.

"Anything?"

Ann was silent. Lucy could see that she had successfully logged into the system.

"You're in?" Lucy sounded hopeful.

"I'm in, but it's scrubbed. If this was my desk, they scrubbed my machine but didn't change the password."

"What about another computer? Can you log in to one of those?"

Ann shifted to the next seat. "Doubtful," she said as she typed in her password. "Each machine would have its own password."

The login attempt failed.

"Nope," Ann said. "Nothing. Dead end."

"Are you sure? There could be something on the hard drive."

"Not allowed. All the information would be stored in the data net-work, but it's probably huge and I don't have any idea where to look or what I'm looking for."

Lucy sighed. They sat in silence for a moment. Ann reached to turn off the computer. Lucy placed her hand on Ann's wrist.

"Wait."

Ann watched while Lucy put her thoughts into words.

"What if you aren't a bad person? What if you got fired because you're a good person?"

Ann smiled a little. "I'd like to think that's the case."

"If the people of this place are evil, and you went against them, they might—"

"Clean out my workstation and put me into a capsule with all of you."

"Then you're not so bad," Lucy said.

Ann chuckled. "Depends on who I pissed off."

"Okay, let's say you pissed 'em off. Would you have taken any pre-cautions? Anything that might help you or anyone else if things went wrong?"

"I would hope so."

"Then you'll have to remember what that might be."

Ann nodded. "Okay. You're right. I'll see if I can think of anything."

"HEY, YOU TWO! COME LOOK AT THIS!" Jill yelled from the lab hallway she was in.

"You keep going here," Lucy said. "I'll see what she wants." Lucy left and walked through the lab to the opposite end where the small hall-way branched away. At the end of the short hall, she found Jill stand-ing in front of a floor-to-ceiling observation window.

"Check that out," Jill said.

The room was partially lit from the combined spillover light from other rooms.

"This is the room next to the capsule room," Lucy said.

"Right, the one with the sliding glass door."

"Is that a table?"

"Not just a table. Look at those restraints. It has little extensions for arms and legs. This is for tying a person down."

"Hard to tell."

"Look at that shelf at the other end. See those black bags on the shelf? Body bags, maybe? And why do they have *two* mops and buckets?"

"Cleaning supplies?"

"Don't be naive. Awful things happen in there. This is human experimentation, and we're the experiments."

"Then how come we're not injured?"

Jill shook her head. "You don't want to face up to it. I understand. But I'll bet what's going on here is illegal. And there's no way we're here of our own free will."

"Stop talking like this."

"We were probably abducted, assuming we weren't born and bred for this."

"Shut up!" Lucy hissed.

"Has the big-boobed one confessed to anything yet?"

"She might have found some—"

"Yeah, yeah. I'm gonna smack it out of her."

Jill tried to step around Lucy. Lucy grabbed Jill by the throat and pushed her against the wall, quick and hard.

"Pretty strong for a girl," Jill said, croaking.

Lucy let her go.

"Ann may have found something," Lucy said. "It's possible she's a victim, too."

"How so?"

"Her desk. It's the only one cleared away. They tried to get rid of her."

"You can't know that."

"Going on instinct."

Jill sighed and shook her head.

"For now, you will leave her alone. Even if she is dirty, she's our only hope, and that's the way it is. Don't get in the way. If there's reckoning, it will come later. Okay?"

Jill nodded. Lucy noticed another locked door behind them.

"I'm not sure I want to see any more rooms," Lucy said.

"Any new room might have a way out."

Lucy called out to Ann, asking for the code she had punched into the other doors. After Ann gave her the number, Lucy put her hand to the keypad to unlock the door. She paused.

"If what you suspect is true, then all of this is off the books. Illegal."

"Yep," Jill said.

"Which means we might be in the middle of nowhere, and the only people who know about us won't be coming to help us. If anything, they'll come to wipe us out."

"If that's the case, I want to at least know who I am before I die."

"Then we'll try to find out."

Lucy keyed in the code. The door clacked open, and they stepped inside. While they explored the new room, Ann sat at the computer, nosing around whatever rudimentary files remained on her hard drive. Mostly dull documents about safety protocols and shipping invoices, cafeteria menu items, and other stuff of little use other than to prove the facility was large and had cafeteria and shipping facilities.

Her frustration grew. She knew this was her desk. There was nothing here to show it was hers, but her instinct screamed that she was close to an answer. She glanced at the other stations. Pictures of women and men hugging and smiling, photos of children at birthday parties. The faces had the ring of familiarity, but she couldn't put names to the faces.

"There has to be something," she said to herself.

"Are we going to be okay?"

Ann spun around at Sara's voice. She stood in the doorway with her arm wrapped around Diana. Ann felt a wave of affection for Sara. She looked so young, her voice so scared.

"I don't know, Hon. Just trying to find answers."

"I'm hungry."

"You might as well check around the drawers and stuff out there. Could be some snacks or water bottles around."

"Is that computer working?" Sara asked.

"It is," Ann said. She anticipated the next question. "And yes, I think it was my computer."

Sara looked more excited than suspicious. "Is there anything there we can use?"

"Not so far. I'll bet I angered whoever runs this place."

"And that's why you were put in with us?"

"Can't say for sure, but it makes sense."

"These are bad people. Were you one of them?"

"Maybe. I like to think I was a good person who got caught up in something bad."

"They punished you. You must have known something. You must have left a sign or a clue in case you got caught."

"Can't find anything."

"There must be something!"

Ann looked around the empty workstation. "I hope so. I'll keep looking."

"I'll see if I can find something to eat."

Sara led Diana back into the capsule room.

Ann looked under her computer monitor, under her keyboard, in the nooks and crannies of the workstation.

"There's got to be something," she said to herself.

She pushed back her chair and crawled under the desk, looking around for anything out of the ordinary, lifting up power cords and computer cords. She was about to crawl out when she saw it.

A piece of paper, folded so many times it was but a small chip, sat between the prongs of a cord plugged into a power strip. Her heart racing, she fetched the paper and unfolded it. Written on the scrap in what Ann was certain was her own handwriting was a lengthy computer file path. C:Documents/Folders/Eve . . . and so on. Under the path were the words "hidden."

So excited she almost fell out of the chair as she sat down, Ann quickly adjusted her settings to make hidden files visible. Then she followed the path, a ridiculously long trail meant to keep something out of accidental view, until she came to the final destination. Taking a breath, she opened it, and discovered a collection of videos. Lucy and Jill stood frozen in this new room, the largest yet. To their left were rows of filing cabinets. To their right were several rows of large, vertical Plexiglass tubes, each one containing a floating body. Each body was female, and all were mostly human. All bore horrible mutations, everything from extra limbs, digits, and heads, to organs on the outside. Some sprouted long, saber-like teeth. Others stared sightlessly through eyes three times too large for the head. Some had arms that reached to the bottom of their tube and folded up. Others had no face. Many suffered unexplainable, yawning cavities in their bodies.

"My God," Lucy said.

"God had nothing to do with this," Jill said, her voice quivering. "This is wannabe God stuff. Playing God."

Lucy pointed at the pitiful victims with a shaking hand. "Is this what we—"

"Don't say it. Don't even think it."

They walked along the rows of bodies, unable to stop themselves from examining the human wreckage on display.

"Why would they keep these?" Jill asked.

"I can't look anymore," Lucy said.

She left the upright tubes and went to the filing cabinets. She opened a drawer and found a collection of file folders.

"There might be answers here," she said.

Jill joined her, opening another drawer to do her own search.

The files contained photos and names of various women.

"Women who work here?" Jill asked.

Lucy shook her head. "Women behind us, I'm guessing."

Jill pointed to a line on the form she studied.

"Look at this."

Lucy looked over her shoulder.

"'Place of Acquisition,'" Jill said. "What does that mean?"

"Where they were taken. Where *we* were taken."

"Or tricked. Who knows?"

Lucy dropped the file she held. She clutched her abdomen and doubled over. Jill put her arms around her.

"What is it? What's wrong?"

"Cramp of some kind," Lucy said. "Damn. Feels like my guts are coming apart."

"Oh my God, I'll get Ann."

Lucy grabbed her arm. "No. It's passing. Let her work."

Jill waited while Lucy caught her breath. The spell appeared to have passed. Jill wiped tears. They both knew, but didn't say, that Lucy's mysterious cramp had something to do with the savaged women behind them.

"If those women are in these files, we might be, too," Jill said.

"Good idea," Lucy said, standing straight and returning to normal. "Let's look around."

"I need to know who I am," Jill said, thumbing through the files with fierce urgency. Back in the lab, Ann clicked open the first video and gasped when her own face appeared on screen, shot with the computer's web cam. Ann was dressed in professional work clothes and a white lab coat. Her hair was up, and she wore reading glasses. A no-nonsense female pro. She spoke in a hushed nonchalant manner to avoid attention.

"I'm out of time," Ann watched herself say. "And if you've found this, so are you."

"The experiment is a failure. What we've done is morally abhorrent. I didn't know in the beginning how bad it was, but as time went by and I learned more and was trusted more, I figured out what a hell we've created.

"The sleep chambers are necessary to let the matrix of the specimens realign. Christ, listen to me. 'Specimens.' I mean *humans*. Human beings. So many lives destroyed. There are files showing their real names. Take them if you can. Their families will at least have closure.

"I sent a message to the outside. I don't know if it was received or if anyone will come or whether they will save us or kill us. There's no outside internet. Get out now. I don't know how you will find your way back to anyone who can help, but you must get those files and leave now. I'm sorry I wasn't strong enough to stop this. I can't speak to the motivations for what's been done here. I only know the world must learn of it so it can't happen again."

Ann's alter ego looked around, paranoid. Absolute fear in her voice and eyes.

"I'm out of time. This is Doctor Karen Eve," she said.

Ann, now Karen, flinched at learning her real name.

The video ended, and Karen sat with her shoulders slumped, stunned.

"So you were a good guy."

Karen whirled around to see Lucy standing behind her.

"You saw all of that?" Karen asked.

"I did, Doctor."

"Then you know I tried to stop it," Karen said. "That they put me in the experiment as punishment. Whatever happens to you will happen to me."

"Can it be stopped?" Lucy asked. "Whatever's going to happen to us. Can it be turned back?"

"I don't know. I didn't have time to record any details. My priority was to warn everyone to get out as soon as possible. I didn't leave any procedure to reverse whatever they've done."

Lucy sighed. "I had a bad cramp back there. Felt like my innards were tying up in knots."

"You okay now?"

"I'm okay, but I feel different. Like puzzle pieces rearranged, you know?"

Karen nodded. "What do you mean, 'back there?'"

Lucy waved for her to follow. "You have to see what Jill and I found."Lucy led Karen to the storage room. Karen felt their gaze hard upon her as she looked at the mangled bodies floating in the clinical lighting overhead. Her breathing quickened, but she did not overreact. An immense sadness overcame her as she walked through the bodies.

"Anything ringing a bell, Ann?" Jill asked.

Karen didn't look at her. "My name is Karen."

Jill, surprised, looked at Lucy.

"She found out who she is," Lucy said.

"What?"

Jill ran to Karen and seized her by the hair. She dragged Karen to the file cabinets and threw her to the ground.

"What right do you have to know who you are?" she screamed. *"You did this to us! I want to know who I am, dammit! And you're going to tell me! Where is my file!"*

Lucy wrestled Jill away from Karen, who remained on the floor, stunned.

Jill, hyperventilating with rage, opened a drawer and pulled out a stack of files. She dumped the files on Karen's head. Manila folders and sheets of paper rained down on her head. Jill tossed two more stacks of files onto Karen before Lucy again restrained her.

"Find my file, bitch."

Karen glared up at Jill and got to her feet. She kicked at a pile of papers.

"Look at those storage containers," she said to Jill. Tell me what you see."

Jill refused to take her eyes off Karen.

"Look!" Karen screamed.

Jill and Lucy both quickly looked.

At the bottom of each container was a crude strip of masking tape. Each strip of tape bore marker writing identifying each body with a name and number: Sara 13, Jill 5, Ann 12, Lucy 4, Diana 9, every name with various numbers.

"At least you're not one of them," Karen said. "Not yet, anyway. Each one of us is part of a series. Look up all the Jills, and see what's led up to you. You might be the perfect one."

"I'm going to kill you," Jill said.

"There might be a trigger that makes these mutations happen," Karen said. "Maybe I'll remember it. Maybe I already do. Either way, it's time for you to shut up. I'm getting out of here. I don't give a damn about the rest of you, but you're welcome to tag along if I find a way out."

Jill rushed forward. Lucy held her back.

"Find your own damn file . . . *Jill*," Karen said.

They watched her stalk out of the storage room. Jill controlled her breathing.

"What are we going to do with her?" she asked.

"Nothing we can do," Lucy said. "She's right. Again, if we have any hope, she's it. And it looks like she's a victim, too. Let's just work together and if we escape, we can go our separate ways."

"She was still a part of it."

"We don't know how these things are run. The left hand might not know what the right is doing."

Jill thought about that.

Lucy walked to the door. "Come on, let's see if there's anything else we can do."

"No." Jill didn't move. "I'm staying here."

She knelt to gather the files.

"I'm going to find my file," she said. "When you find a way out, let me know."

Lucy left her to her search. Lucy returned to the lab to find Sara, naked again, climbing into the rectangular, glass, tanning bed-like device she had earlier examined with Jill. Karen helped Sara step into the thing. Once inside, Sara laid down. Karen placed a small oxygen mask over her mouth and nose and closed the lid. Diana sat in Karen's computer chair.

Lucy stood next to the mechanism and looked at Sara.

"What is this thing?"

"I can't remember," Karen said.

"How do you know it won't hurt her?"

"I'm pretty sure it won't."

"You're going on instinct again?"

"Yes. My guess is this thing is an examining tool," Karen said. "If I'm right, it might tell us something about who we are."

"Or what we are."

"That too."

Karen keyed in a code, and the machine hummed to life. The glass and plastic walls of the device glowed blue. A tube led from the gadget's support platform and into the closed bed where Sara lay. From there, a clear, thick gel oozed into the box, first collecting at her feet, then making its way up her legs. Sara tried to shrink away from the gel, but there was little room to move.

"Can she breathe?" Lucy asked.

"She has oxygen."

Sara's eyes met Lucy's. Lucy saw not pleading for rescue, but a request to watch over her should something go wrong.

The gel rapidly filled the capsule, covering her body until it rose above her face and filled the enclosure. Sara thrashed a little as she was submerged, but calmed when she realized she could breathe.

"Now what?" Lucy asked.

"Now we see what this thing does," Karen said.

Lucy noticed something sparkling in the gel.

"What's that? Looks like glitter in that stuff."

Karen leaned in for a closer look.

"I'll be damned," she said.

"What?"

"I think they're nanobots. Little robots. They swim around the gel and check everything."

Sara flinched once, then again. Lucy saw flashes of pain on her face.

"What are they doing to her?"

"Taking blood, probably. She'll be okay," Karen said. "This is good. We might get answers."

In less than five minutes, the nanobot-infused gel had done its work and was sucked away by the tube. When it was empty again, Karen lifted the lid, and they helped Sara out. The gel had left her hair and skin dry.

"You okay?" Karen asked.

"That was freaky," Sara said.

"Did it hurt?" Lucy asked.

"Only for a second," Sara said. "It was like I was getting felt up or something."

"It was an examination," Karen said. "That gel doesn't have much of a bedside manner, I'm afraid."

"So now what?" Lucy asked.

The machine hummed again. There was a brief whine and clattering sound, and a paper card spat out into a receiving tray. Everyone looked at the paper.

"Now we get the results." They stared at the sheet of paper. Sara got dressed.

"Well? Are you going to read it?" Lucy asked.

Karen took the paper from the tray, but didn't read it.

"Let's test everyone first. Then compare," she said. "Might be easier to interpret that way."

Lucy doffed her clothes. "Me next. I want to get this over with."

When Lucy finished, they helped a jittery Diana into the machine. Karen took her turn before they called in Jill, who refused to enter until Karen stood on the far side of the room and Lucy ran the controls. By the time everyone had taken a turn, they were exhausted. They moved to the capsule room and sat on the floor as Karen reviewed the printed reports. Jill returned to the storage room to continue her search for her personal file.

"I'm tired," Sara said, yawning. "How long did that take?"

They looked at each other.

"What time is it, anyway?" Lucy asked.

Nobody knew.

"Didn't think to wonder about that," Karen said.

There wasn't a clock to be found.

"Maybe the computer has the time?" Karen asked. "It's still booted up if anyone wants to check."

"I'll do it." Lucy stood, stretched, and went into the lab. She returned in seconds.

"Well, it looks like a clock on the lower right of the screen, but I can't read it. It's not English."

"Some other language?" Sara asked.

"Symbols, more like it. If I know what it is, I don't remember," Lucy said. "I can tell it's keeping time by the way it counts and changes over. I can tell it's supposed to be hours, minutes, and seconds, but other than that . . ."

Sara rubbed her temples. "Ugh. When will this nightmare end?"

"Anything on those printouts?" Lucy asked.

Karen looked up. "Can someone get Jill?"

When Lucy returned with Jill, Karen cleared her throat.

"This is pretty straightforward, I think," she said. She showed them the form. "This is like a basic physical. Blood tests. Blood pressure. Heart rate. The works. The little pricks of pain you felt were the little nanobots entering your skin and leaving again. What interests us is this section at the top."

She pointed. They all leaned in to see.

"There are three lines. One says 'Normal Human Composition.' All of us have a zero percent rating on that option."

Unease rippled through the group.

"So we're not human?" Jill asked. "Is that what that means?"

"The second choice is 'Hybrid,'" Karen said, ignoring Jill. "Again, all zero."

"Not even half human," Lucy said.

Sara wept. "This is not going anywhere good."

"Will you cut to the chase already?" Jill asked in a growl.

Karen was grim, but still calm.

"The last option is 'Converged.' We all have a 100% reading for that." She let that sink it and waited for reactions.

"Don't sit there in silence and make us ask you what that means," Lucy said.

"I don't know this for sure, but my guess is 'Converged' means whatever experiment took place here . . . was a success."

"You mean us?" Sara asked.

"Yes."

"So they did whatever they were trying to do?" Jill asked.

"Again, a guess, but I think so. We're the final stage of . . . whatever."

"But what did they do?" Sara asked. "Aren't we just normal women?"

The others stared at her with widening eyes. Diana shrank away, covering her eyes.

"What?" Sara asked. "Look at the writing on your arm," Lucy said.

Sara looked down to see the symbols on her forearm rearranging as if animated. They merged and formed new shapes.

"What's happening?" she asked, weeping. "What's hap—"

She fell to the ground in the grip of a seizure. The others rushed to her, trying to help.

"What's wrong with her?" Jill shouted to Karen.

"I don't know!"

"Help her!" Jill said.

Sara's skin rippled in waves along her limbs. Her eyes rolled up white. Diana curled into a ball as the others shouted and argued. They went to Sara's side and tried to calm her.

"What do we do?" Lucy asked.

"Let's get her into the exam room!" Karen said.

She ran to the keypad and the sliding door whisked open. Lucy carried Sara by the arms; Jill by the legs. Sara's thrashing made her difficult to handle, and they dropped her twice before they got her in the door.

"On the table!" Karen said.

Lucy and Jill exchanged a quick glance, each remembering their uneasiness about this room.

Sara's skin erupted in small bubbles. The bubbles burst to reveal tiny, metallic plates.

"What the hell is this?" Lucy asked.

As they lifted her to the table, Sara's foot shot out, kicking Jill and knocking her to the floor. Jill got to her feet, clutching her abdomen, and saw Lucy and Karen looking at Sara's leg in shock.

Sara's lower leg had grown twelve inches in seconds. The shin bone had extended, neatly separating the flesh at mid-calf and leaving a section of white bone visible. Her foot sat at the end of her leg bone like a grisly shoe. Sara wailed in anguish at the sudden mutation.

Lucy and Karen added their screams to Sara's, both in horror at her suffering and fear for their own futures.

"Get her on the table, quick!" Karen said as they lifted Sara to the table and restrained her arms. They weren't sure what to so with her mutating leg, so they left it free to kick around.

"Now what?" Lucy asked.

"We need to kill her," Jill said.

The others stared at her, mouths agape, while Sara wildly shook her head.

"No!" Lucy shouted.

"We can't let her turn into one of those things!" Jill said.

Sara's arm extended as her leg had. She screamed anew. Jill ran to the counter and searched through the cupboards and drawers.

"I'm going to end this," she said.

Karen ran after her and grabbed her from behind. Jill shook free with an angry grunt, turned and punched Karen in the chin. The more athletic Jill pummeled Karen until Lucy pulled her off. Karen lay on the floor shaking her head, trying to get her senses back. Lucy was too stunned to move. Sara continued to contort and scream. Jill returned to her search and found what she looked for—a scalpel. "No!" Karen shouted, sounding drunk from her beating. "Lucy don't let her!"

But Jill had already pulled the blade across Sara's neck, unleashing a spill of blood. Jill cradled Sara's face in her hands.

"I'm so sorry," Jill said, weeping.

Karen struggled to her feet and tried to reach something that might stop the blood flow. Jill blocked her way.

"Lucy?" Karen pleaded.

Lucy shook her head. "I'm with Jill. We need to stop this."

Sara stopped struggling after minutes that seemed like hours. Then she was still, her eyes staring past the ceiling and into whatever lay beyond. Her arms, legs, even abdomen were in varying stages of elongating, with parts of her skeleton exposed. For a long time, nobody spoke.

"Is this what you'll do to us?" Karen asked.

"I haven't decided," Jill said. "Maybe it's what should be done."

Karen nodded and looked at Lucy.

"What about you? You going to let her cut your throat?"

Lucy stayed silent, but she shot a look of warning to Jill.

"Do you know what was happening to her?" Jill asked.

Karen looked over Sara's mangled body.

"She was metamorphosing."

"What does that mean?" Lucy asked.

"She was turning into another form of life."

"Like a butterfly?" Lucy asked.

"Yeah."

"Nonsense," Jill said. "Your sick experiments were killing her. She was turning into a mutant."

"Mutating, yes, but not in a grotesque way."

"How the hell do you know that?"

Karen pointed to Sara's leg. "This was where the mutation began. The shin bone suddenly grew longer, and it pulled the flesh apart."

"We all saw that," Lucy said.

"Yeah, but look closer," Karen said.

The others leaned in.

Karen pointed to blood vessels that now reached between the flesh of the upper leg and the foot, spanning the the new section of bone.

"Those are blood vessels. You can also see muscle fibers working their way across the exposed bone. All of this in a matter of seconds."

"What are you saying?" Lucy asked.

"She was reassembling!" Karen shouted. "Her skeleton was growing to accommodate new flesh." She glared at Jill. "But you killed her before she could complete the change."

Jill shook her head, stunned. "No. No, you can't know that. Those things in the jars—"

"Were first steps in the process," Karen said. "You saw the results of our exams. We are converged. The last phase. Congrats, Jill. You're a killer."

Karen left the room. Lucy and Jill shared a look, then followed.

"I only did what I thought was best," Jill said.

"In that case, congratulations."

"Don't be a smartass. I'm still not sure I did the wrong thing, even if this experiment worked. I mean, what would she have been?"

"Couldn't say," Karen said.

"Then we're still in the dark," Lucy said.

She went to Diana and sat next to her, putting her arm around her and consoling her.

"You mentioned 'hybrid' earlier," Jill said. "Is that a phase we passed through? A hybrid of human and . . . what, exactly?"

"I'm not sure," Karen said. "Could be animals. Could be . . ."

"Aliens," Lucy said with a snort.

"Again, I don't know."

"I was joking, for God's sake."

Karen shrugged. "I don't know.""This is unbelievable," Jill said.

"It's unbelievable, but it's our reality now," Lucy said. "And no matter what I am now, I will make it through to the end. I want to escape and live my life again."

"I'd like that, too," Karen said.

Jill shrugged. "Fine."

"No more killing," Lucy said. "Not unless we ask for it. Jill?"

"Fine," she said again. "But if I'm going to be turned into some Frankenstein's monster, I want to know who I am. So I'm back to my file search."

She left Karen and Lucy alone.

"What should we do now?" Lucy asked.

"I should examine Sara's body. See if I can learn anything."

"What can I do?"

"Maybe look around some more? Find other rooms we missed? A way out?"

"Okay." Lucy said, turning to Diana. "Honey, you wait here okay? I'm going to look around. You'll be fine."

Lucy left to check the lab. Karen looked at Diana, who stared at the floor with wide, fearful eyes.

"I know you," Karen said. "But how? Did we work together?"

Diana didn't seem to hear.

"Were we made prisoners of our own science? Was I the boss? Were you?"

Diana rocked on her tush, hugging her knees.

"I guess it doesn't matter now," Karen said. "I'll be in the exam room. It's straight ahead. You'll be able to see me through the glass."

Again no answer.

Karen entered the exam room, surprised to see Sara's metamorphosis had advanced, even after her death. The flesh around the elongated leg had advanced.

Sara's mouth, still open wide in her final screams, had new rows of sharp teeth. The vampiric incisors were twice as long as the other teeth. The eyes were centered with fiery irises that looked into unknown spectrums. Talons had sprouted through shredded fingernails and toe-nails. She lifted Sara's arms and wasn't surprised to find the elbow joint now swung both ways.

"A superpredator," Karen said to herself. "Almost, anyway."

Physically lethal, but what of her mindset? Would Sara's gentle personality remained? Or would that have mutated, too? If her mind had assumed the predatory nature of her body, none of them would have survived.

Sara's bubbled skin left a new texture. Karen examined it closely. It was unlike any skin she had ever seen—a leathery armor with a slight golden glow. Certainly not human. If it was animal skin, she didn't recognize it. Although she couldn't prove it, Karen felt a growing conviction that Sara had become part alien. Lucy walked around the lab, scanning the walls and looking into cupboards, searching for any sign of a secret or overlooked entrance. She heard files and papers thrown around in the storage room and grinned at Jill's obsessive quest to learn her real name.

She walked past the examination device they had been in, then circled back to the wall by the door next to the workstations. It was then she saw the door, almost right next to Karen's desk. There was no window, and the card-swipe lock and door handle were the same color as the wall. Easy to miss. They had overlooked it.

Deciding against telling the others, Lucy went to the door and tugged at the handle. Locked. Calling for Karen would do no good. The swipe lock demanded a security card. Her instinct told her answers lay beyond the door, but there was no way in. Her frustration boiled over, the weight of fear and unanswered questions pressed in upon her, and she fought back tears.

"The damn door," she said to herself, furious. *"This goddamn door!"*

A wrenching squeal startled her back to a normal state of mind. The door stood open. The deadbolt had pushed through the metal door frame, splitting it apart as it did so. Shocked, Lucy pulled the door open, nervous to see what waited on the other side, what person or creature could force a deadbolt in such a way.

She crept into the room. Motion-activated lights illuminated a spacious, empty office. Lucy looked around in disbelief. She looked back at the open door and realized—somehow, she had forced the door open with her mind. It was no surprise; all sorts of new things were happening with their bodies and minds. But *how* had she done it?

It was an angry, anguished emotion—focused power—that had caused the door to burst open. She stared at the door and concentrated her thoughts as hard as she could manage. The door opened further and banged against the outer wall. Lucy caught her breath. Telekinesis. A good power to have if needed.

With newfound confidence she explored the office. A typical administrator's desk sat against the wall. The nameplate read: Margaret Singer. Lucy didn't know the name. Laying across the back of the office chair was a white lab coat.

Lucy walked around the desk to examine it. A name tag pinned to the pocket had the same name. She searched the pockets and her heart skipped when she found a swipe card. She gasped when she saw the picture on the card, smiling above the name.

It was Diana. "What is it?"

Lucy yelped at the sound of Jill's voice.

"Dammit! Make some noise when you walk!"

"Sorry," Jill said, walking into the office. "I needed a break. My back is killing me. What's all of this?"

"Boss's office, I'm guessing," Lucy said.

"Margaret Singer," Jill said, reading the name plate. "She's not here I take it?"

Lucy shook her head. "She's out in the capsule room."

Jill's eyes went wide. "Who?"

Lucy held out the security card. Jill saw Diana's face.

"I'll be damned."

"Diana, or Margaret I mean, is the one in charge. Or was. She knows everything."

"Yeah, except her brain is shot from the capsule," Jill said. "We'll get nothing. She's not even responsible anymore."

"I just want out of here," Lucy said. "There aren't any answers. Only questions. I have a feeling it was set up that way."

Jill looked around. "Doesn't look like they kept much in here. There's a computer, but I doubt Karen could get into the boss's computer."

"How does the boss end up in the capsule?" Lucy asked.

"There was an uprising. A mutiny, you know?"

Lucy nodded. "Margaret and Karen were the losers . . ."

"But on the side of good or evil?"

"And do people like this have such a distinction? Maybe it was just a power struggle."

They stood in the office, wondering what the next move should be.

"What's in there?" Jill asked.

"Where?"

Jill pointed to a door set into the far wall. Like the office door, it was the same color as the wall and inconspicuous. Seeing Lucy hadn't noticed it, she walked to it and pushed on it.

"No lock. No handle," Jill said. "How the hell do they get in?"

"Let me try," Lucy said.

Lucy put her shoulder to the door. Not yet ready to give away her newfound powers of the mind, she rammed her shoulder into the door as cover for her mind smashing it in. Lucy stood in the open doorway with a smile and gestured Jill to enter.

"Damn," Jill said. "Your strength is already pumping up."

They entered the room and froze.

"What the hell is this?" Jill asked, gasping.

It was a chapel, with crude, wooden benches arranged in a circle around an altar. Scarlet drapes and carpets covered the walls and floors.

"Look at those symbols on the drapes," Lucy said, pointing from the drapes to her skin. "Same as those on our bodies."

"It's a church," Jill said.

"I know my memory is hazy, but I'm sure a church ought to have crosses. Not whatever this stuff is."

"They weren't just doing experiments. We're part of some kind of worship. We're in deep shit."

"We have got to get out of here. That should be our only priority."

"Not until I find out who I am."

"You're obsessed with that, and I understand. But I've got a bad feeling we're on a ticking clock," Lucy said. "Maybe there are answers outside of this place. We can go to the police."

"I have to know."

Jill left the room. Lucy watched, disbelieving. She stared at the swipe card in her hand. Should she tell Karen about this? Or just try to use it? She didn't think she had a choice. Lucy gave the office one last look-through before she left. She chuckled to herself in spite of everything because the desk was so mundane compared to the high weirdness in the chapel room. Maybe such compartmentalization was necessary for scientists who worship strange beings.

She glanced at the mangled deadbolt of the office door as she passed. Two doors forced open with the powers of her mind, the resistance of metal and wood easy to overcome.

Diana looked up fearfully as Lucy entered the capsule room. Lucy gave her a reassuring smile, then stared at the sliding glass door that cut them off from the rest of the facility. The access button had been sabotaged.

"It might get noisy for a few seconds, Hon," she said to Diana. "It'll be okay."

Diana curled up and was silent.

Lucy concentrated on the door, imagining it open. Willing it to do so. A high-pitched metallic squeal rang out as the door inched to the left, moved by unseen forces powered by Lucy's changing brain. As the track of the door resisted, the squeal turned into a grinding chug and pop of breaking metal parts.

Karen came out of the examination room, her eyes and mouth open wide at Lucy's ability.

When the door was open, Lucy buckled the door frame and warped the track so it couldn't close again. She sat on the security desk and caught her breath.

Karen examined the door and looked at Lucy, who grinned.

"Telekinesis?"

Lucy nodded.

"Must be one of the powers we've been 'gifted' with," Karen said.

"You sure you don't know where this is taking us?" Lucy asked.

"I honestly don't. But maybe it won't be bad. What if we're meant to do good in the world?"

"I guess. But what kind of world is it? What is good? What is evil? Will our minds be the same when we turn? Mental power like this can kill people."

"I know."

"Kill them *easily*."

"Yes, *I know*."

Lucy stood and stretched, her breathing back to normal.

"Did you learn anything about Sara?"

Karen shook her head. "Only confirmed what was obvious after she died. The metamorphosis breaks and destroys our normal bodies, then quickly rebuilds in the new matrix. A very painful process, but fast."

"Could the new body rebuild when wounded?"

"Most likely. Jill had perfect timing with that scalpel. A few seconds later and I'm guessing the cut might have healed instantly."

"So Sara would have lived? We'll be immortal?"

"But not invincible. Most wounds will heal. Massive trauma, no."

"So slashes and gunshots, yes."

"Bombs and dismemberment, probably not."

They heard Diana's fearful grunts, and went to her side, calming her.

"How much time do you think we have?" Lucy asked.

"No idea. Could happen to any of us at any second."

Lucy looked at Diana and stroked her hair.

"I know who she is," Lucy said.

Karen looked surprised, then figured it out.

"She works here, doesn't she?"

Lucy nodded. "Margaret Singer. Not only does she work here, she's the boss."Karen frowned. "How did the boss end up in the experiment? How and *why* did it happen?"

"You should go into her office. Take a good look around."

"Where is it?"

"Go past the workstations. There's a door we missed. It's open."

Karen left to check it out. Lucy stayed with Diana, keeping her arm around her. She studied the older woman's skin. The symbols appeared to jitter and move, but Lucy dismissed it as a twitch of skin.

Karen returned, looking pale.

"Well, that's disturbing," she said.

"Ring any bells?"

"No. Doesn't look like any religion I remember. At least I hope the hell not."

"This is a secret experiment. Would I be in the ballpark to say that? Off the books?"

Karen nodded.

"We need to watch her close," Karen said. "She might have put herself into the capsule knowing the metamorphosis would work."

"What should we do with her?"

"Are you implying—"

"Maybe we should keep her someplace that'll keep her and us safe, is what I'm implying."

Karen picked up her train of thought. "Let's get her into the exam room."

After Karen unshackled Sara's body from the exam table, she dragged the body into the lab while Lucy covered Diana's eyes. Karen then cleaned off the table. When all was ready, they led Diana into the exam room and helped her onto the table. Diana whimpered in fear, but did not resist. Her limbs tensed as they restrained her wrists and ankles.

"It's going to be okay, Sweetie," Lucy said.

Diana wildly shook her head.

"We won't hurt you, this is just in case," Karen said, patting her cheek.

Diana did not calm down.

"Is there anything we can cover her with?" Lucy asked.

Karen checked the cupboard until she found a thin blanket. They placed it over Diana and tucked it under her chin. Cozied up under the blanket, she stopped struggling. Her breathing was still fast, but she was calm.

"It's okay," Lucy said, running her fingers through Diana's hair. "Just rest now. We'll be right back."

Lucy and Karen returned to the capsule room and stood at the wrenched-open sliding door.

"Shall we?" Lucy asked.

Karen nodded, and they stepped into the dark hallway. A few steps into the blackness, the overhead lights flickered on, each successive light coming on as they passed under it. When the third light came on, it revealed a hallway entrance several feet ahead to the left. They paused, looked at each other, and went to to the entrance.

They turned into the hallway and found a female security guard lying still on the floor. Karen gasped and Lucy jumped. They stood frozen, staring at the body.

"Hello?" Karen called out in a quivering voice.

They looked at each other.

"We've got to keep going, no matter what we find," Lucy said.

They moved forward together, kneeling at the body.

The woman had blond hair, pulled back tight. Her skin was pale, and her eyes had the blank, glazed look of someone who faded painfully into death.

"She's been shot," Karen said.

Bloodstains soaked a wide radius around two wounds—one in the heart, one in the abdomen. A pistol rested near her right hand. Karen checked her pulse.

"Dead for sure."

Lucy shook her head. "Whatever we find just makes it more confusing."

Karen scanned the hallway. "There's a door at the end. Open."

They went to the door and looked in. It was dark. Karen waved her hands, and the lights came on along with a computer control panel with several small television screens along the wall. Half of the screens were dark, the others were security feeds to the lab, capsule room, and other areas the women had already explored.

"Security office," Lucy said. "Look at the screens," Lucy said. "We can see the lab."

"Why are some of them dark?"

"The lights are out in the other areas, I guess."

They looked around the small room. A padlocked weapons cabinet sat opposite the door. There were janitorial supplies in a corner. Opposite the weapons was a large facility map hanging on the wall. The women studied it, following the hallway and room layouts with their fingers and orienting to their location.

"We are here," Karen said. "Now what?"

"I guess we should check those other areas. Look for survivors."

Karen gestured toward the high-tech security desk. "Can we learn anything from this?"

Lucy sat at the desk and touched the display screen. She smiled when it glowed to life.

"Awesome. I'll check for a security recording," Lucy said. "Maybe I can learn what happened. How long do you think we were in those capsules?"

"Hard to say. Considering it's a quick process and that we could go without nutrition and water for only so long? I'd say a day. Two at the most."

"All right. I'll go back two days and watch what happened."

"I can check the other areas. If someone recognizes me, I might be okay."

"Good idea. And be careful."

"What about Jill?" Karen asked.

"Leave her. She's unpredictable right now. Best to leave her to the file search. Maybe she'll find out who the rest of us are."

"Okay, then."

Karen stepped back into the hallway. She would have to walk past the dead guard again. Holding her breath, she tip-toed past the corpse as if it might grab her ankle. She saw the pistol lying on the floor. A weapon might come in handy, if she could figure out how to use it. She rushed back and picked it up. It felt heavy, dangerous, and safe.

Lucy tapped the large touch screen, poking around the security files and narrowing down her choices until she found files labeled as a surveillance archive. Assuming each file represented one day, she counted back two from the most recent file and opened it.

The recording playback overrode the live feeds, and all the cameras showed the recording for their respective areas. The lab sections were on the right side of the screen bank. Lucy spotted the capsule room. She had to look close, but confirmed that only three capsules were occupied—herself, Jill, and Sara. Karen and Margaret had yet to be put in.

She activated the visual search, and the feed rushed ahead. Employees in lab coats darted about in fast-motion, including Dr. Karen Eve. Karen worked at her station, talked with co-workers, and seemed at home. When Dr. Margaret Singer and two men in lab coats surrounded Karen at her workstation, Lucy slowed the recording to normal speed.

Karen's reactions to Singer and the men showed defensiveness and fear. They appeared to accuse her of something. Other employees left their desks and cleared the room. The men grabbed Karen by the arms as her screams—mute on the recording—went unheeded. They dragged her from the lab and into Margaret's office and Lucy shifted her gaze to that room's camera.

The men roughly stripped off Karen's clothes until she was naked. Margaret prepared an injection. Lucy covered her mouth, fearing what she was about to see. Karen flailed in panic, as if she knew what was to come. The men held her tight as Margaret gave the shot into Karen's buttocks. The men then dragged her off camera toward the temple room. Lucy looked for the temple room feed, unsurprised to discover there was no camera in that room.

Taking a deep breath, Lucy fast-forwarded until Margaret appeared again, followed by the men pulling Karen by the arms. She was still naked, only now adorned with the symbol writing on her skin. Karen moved slowly, obviously drugged, and offered no resistance as they placed her in the capsule. Margaret attached the required tubes and wires. They closed the lid. Margaret entered commands into the control panel. Lucy was about to fast-forward, when Margaret and the two men extended their hands to each other, forming a triangle over the capsule. They prayed or chanted, then went on with their business, looking bored. Karen entered the main hallway again. The lights flickered on as she passed through new areas. Another guard lay dead on the floor, shot many times. A second body, this one clad in snow camouflage fatigues, lay further on. Two other dead soldiers in the snow fatigues lay in the next section of hallway. Bullet holes perforated the walls.

A mangled security door marked the end of the hall. She crept around the broken glass and found herself in a blank, empty corridor. She guessed it to be a connective passage. It ran to her left and right. She went right and emerged into a reception area. There were numerous offices here. Plenty of desks and office equipment. A security booth stood near what Karen assumed to be the main entrance. If the lab was the heart and soul of the building's purpose, this was the administrative part. The worker ants.

Those ants now lay dead and scattered throughout the room, sprawled on the floor and dangled limp over chairs and desks. The receptionist still sat at her desk. She leaned back in her chair, staring at the ceiling through sightless eyes, a bullet hole in her forehead. The first to die in the attack.

The battle had been fierce and destructive. Men and women in civilian clothing, riddled with bullet wounds, covered the floor and furniture. Soldiers and security guards were among the dead.

Karen worked to control her breathing. Her stomach was empty, but she felt the urge to heave. She fought it down. She swept her gun around the room as she looked for any sign someone might have survived, worried someone might rise up and try to kill her with their last burst of energy.

That she and the other women were the main target of this attack was obvious. She had tried to report the activities of the lab to outside authorities. Had her report brought this response? She put the thought out of her mind.

No one had survived the massacre in the administrative section. None of the faces jogged her memory. The front entrance was locked. How the soldiers got in she didn't know.

She returned to the connecting corridor and followed it to the other end. There she discovered living quarters for the workers. There were bunks, a cafeteria, a library, a gym and shower facilities. In every area she found dead bodies. The invading soldiers found no resistance here. People had been shot eating meals, napping, showering, and sleeping.

Another forced security door stood open near the employee living area. She walked through it and down the hall. There were five rooms with swipe locks. A nameplate marked each door. The names were Sara, Lucy, Ann, Jill, and Diana. Karen shook as she read the names. She nudged open the first door—Ann's door—and saw a young girl laying dead on her bed, shot to death. She wore a white hospital gown. The other rooms were filled with dead young women.

"Replacements," Karen muttered.

Satisfied that everyone but herself, Lucy, Jill, and Diana were the only living people in the place, she made her way back to Lucy. As she passed through the connecting corridor she saw an opening in the wall. Hidden by the bright lights and white paint, one could pass by it without noticing.

Raising her weapon again, Karen walked into the opening, which led her through a zig-zagging maze of abrupt right and left turns until she came to a vast chamber. The size of the room was out of proportion to the cramped spaces of the rest of the facility. A domed roof made of beveled glass revealed stars in the night sky.

Benches surrounded a center altar. Symbols of unknown meaning decorated the walls. When Karen compared them to those on her skin, they were a match. A star map covered a section of the wall. It was not the solar system, but a star pattern she either didn't know or couldn't remember. One planet was circled and singled out for special attention. More rune writing surrounded the planet.

Overwhelmed and exhausted, Karen sat on a bench to rest. In the security office, Lucy again sped through the video feed as things returned to normal after Karen had been coerced into the experiment. It didn't take long for more strange events to make her slow the playback once more. There was sudden panic as Margaret burst from her office, shouting at people. In the lab and in the administrative areas people scrambled in response to Margaret's orders when soldiers burst in through the front entrance.

Lucy flinched as she watched the invaders gun down everyone they found. Staff security did the best they could to resist. Lucy found it interesting that they concentrated their efforts on defending the entrance to the lab, allowing the soldiers to wipe out those they found in the living areas. It was in the lab hallway that the last of the soldiers and security officers fought until all combatants lay dead.

As the battle played out on the security screens, Margaret disappeared from her office with a blonde-haired female guard, the one they found dead in the hall. Presumably, they had gone into the temple, for when they appeared again, Margaret was naked and covered in writing. She was alert and in charge, not drugged. With the guard aiding her, they moved fast. Margaret crawled into the final capsule as the guard followed her instructions, attaching wires and tubes and keying in commands on the console. She lowered the lid and Margaret was sealed in. The guard raised her arms in prayer, then drew her weapon and ran to the hallway. It was there that she joined the fight to defend the experiment. She was shot, though, and stumbled into the hallway where she collapsed and died.

After the guard died, all was still in the facility. The motion lights eventually shut down, going dark one by one. She fast-forwarded until Jill's capsule opened. Lucy watched her walk around the room, trying to make sense of it all. She did nothing suspicious. In seconds, the other lids opened, and events caught up to where they had started for Lucy and the others.

"We were supposed to die," Karen said.

Lucy yelped in surprise. "Dammit!"

"I guess it's my fault. I sent a message, and this was the reply."

They shared what they discovered, then sat in silence to process.

"Soldiers invade from outside and fight against soldiers from inside," Lucy said."Damn good security guards here," Karen said. They're the only reason we're alive."

"Did they save us out of love for their fellow man? Or to preserve the experiment?"

"To preserve the experiment," Karen said. "And to complete the ritual."

Lucy folded her arms. "I don't like that word."

"I found a temple room," Karen said.

"Like the one in the office?"

"Only more grand. These people worshiped a being from another planet."

"That's what Sara was turning into," Lucy said. "An alien."

"A hybrid. A perfect human/alien hybrid," Karen said, laughing bitterly. "Congrats, Lucy. We've made history."

"So these scientists give the aliens a hybrid. For what purpose? To take over planet Earth? And what would the scientists get in return?"

"Nothing sounds crazy anymore."

"So who came to kill us?" Lucy asked. "I thought this was a government project."

"There must be competing factions. Internal struggles, you know?"

"So what happens when they don't hear back from their kill squad?"

"They send another? Only bigger?"

Lucy stood. "We have to get out of here. Did you find a way out?"

"I found the entrance. Looks locked up solid."

"Not a problem," Lucy said. "Let's get the others and go."

They rushed back through the capsule room. Lucy glanced into the exam room as they passed. Diana didn't see them.

"What about Diana?" Lucy asked. "Should we take her with us?"

"Might be too risky."

"I don't think I could live with myself if we leave her."

"Let's see what Jill thinks."

They threaded their way back to the specimen room, where Jill still pawed through file after file, her eyes ablaze with obsession.

"We have to go," Karen said.

"I'm busy," Jill said.

"Now, Jill," Lucy said. "There were gun fights all over the facility."

"Glad I slept through it."

"They came to kill *us*, but the security guards stopped them before they died. Everyone's dead but us."

Jill stood up. "So you found something?"

"We'll tell you on the way," Karen said. "More soldiers could be back anytime."

Jill hesitated, looking at the remaining file drawers.

"If you stay here you'll die for sure," Lucy said.

Jill cursed under her breath. "All right. Let's go."

"Wait," Lucy said. "What about Diana? I mean Margaret."

"She's responsible for turning us into things. To hell with her," Jill said.

"I'm with Jill," Karen said. "I know Diana is brain-damaged, but she might not be when she turns. She's a monster."

"Okay, then," Lucy said. "Let's go. The front door is on the other side of the building."

They ran through the lab and out into the specimen room. Lucy, running ahead, screamed and slid to a stop. The other two collided with her. Everyone gasped when they saw Diana—Margaret—standing in the capsule room. She was seven feet tall. Her teeth long and sharp. Her eyes fiery red. Talons on the end of her hands and feet. Her skin a shimmering gold hide of tiny organic metal squares.

"My sisters," she said, in a lucid, calm voice. "Please don't leave me."Lucy, Karen, and Jill stood frozen before the towering creature. Despite the overwhelming predatory terror of her appearance, Diana, aka Dr. Margaret Singer, was perfection and beauty. In this unknown place, she was no more an outcast or mutant than they were. In whatever home world this creature belonged to, she was exalted above others.

"My looks are only the beginning of my perfection, sisters," Margaret said. "And it belongs to all of us."

The three women exchanged looks. Nobody knew what to say.

"You have questions," Margaret said.

She strolled around the capsule room with long, elegant strides.

"You are on Earth," she said, as if answering an unheard question.

Lucy jolted, knowing Margaret had heard the question in her mind.

"And you," Margaret said, fixing her feline gaze on Jill. "Are nobody who will be missed out there."

Jill's breathing quickened. Tears gathered at the corners of her eyes.

"Yeah, well screw you."

Margaret bared her teeth with a purring laugh.

"Don't be angry. You are only moments away from perfection. You will not miss your old life." She looked at Karen. "You've been quiet. A silent posture is best for a traitor like you. You deserve a coward's death, but I have mercy, and I have granted you eternal life with us. The metamorphosis should clear the confusion in your brain. If not, well . . ."

"The alien genes we used. Where are they from?" Karen asked.

"It is not for me to tell you. Soon we will commune with the Great Ones. To commune with them is to know everything."

"So what are we waiting for?" Jill asked.

"For you to change. It is only minutes away."

Margaret waved her long, deadly limbs in the air, admiring their strength and beauty. The other women watched her in fear. There was no point in moving or trying to escape.

"That's right," Margaret said, reading minds again. "I am the ultimate predator. Greater than any lion, shark . . . or human."

"Is that why?" Lucy asked. "All of this was to make us predators? For what purpose?"

"The subjugation of this planet."

"Just the four of us?"

"It was supposed to be five," Margaret said, glaring at Jill, who looked away. "But four will be enough to start."

"What if we don't want to?" Karen asked.

"Then you can die now," Margaret said. "You plan to kill me after you transform. You should know your mind will transform as well. We will rule, my sisters! Ah, peace is coming to our troubled world!"

Her expression of elation narrowed to a sour looked that she fixed on Karen.

"So? Will you die or transform?"

"I never wanted to be part of this. Count me out."

Lucy and Jill stepped away from Karen without realizing they had done it.

Margaret's expression was even. "Very well." Margaret stretched out her hand. The spikes on the ends of her fingers extended into obsidian talons. She waved them in the air.

"Wait!" Lucy said. "You don't have to do this! There has to be a compromise!"

Karen closed her eyes.

"Hoping for a quick death?" Margaret chuckled, ignoring Lucy. "I have more experimenting I can do with you."

She clutched Karen by they throat and lifted her into the air. Margaret glanced at Lucy and Jill.

"Watch this and decide which side you're on."

She plunged the talons into Karen's gut. Karen opened her mouth in shock, but it was Margaret who screamed.

Karen fell to the ground, holding her bleeding abdomen. Margaret stumbled backward, flailing her arms and tripping over her own legs. Her screams were unearthly.

Lucy and Jill ran to Karen and watched as Margaret thrashed in a ferocious seizure. Her head whipped back and forth so fast it was a gray blur. Her screams descended into the guttural clicks and grunts of an unknown language.

They flinched as a loud crack rang out. Margaret folded in half. Her cries continued as first her arms, then her legs, cracked and accordioned toward her torso, as if her trunk sucked in the outer limbs. The spine cracked two more times. Margaret's cries and grunts went silent. The massive creature had compressed and drawn into a grotesque mass of bleeding and broken limbs. Margaret was dead.

"Will that happen to us?" Lucy asked.

"Not likely," Karen said, gasping. "She wasn't really part of the experiment. Neither was I. You two are safe. Not sure what lies ahead for me."

Only mildly comforted, Lucy and Jill pulled away from the shock of Margaret's disintegration to treat Karen's wounds.

"How deep?" Lucy asked.

"Pretty deep," Karen said, hissing through clenched teeth. "Not good."

Jill stood and ran toward the exam room. "I'll get something to stop the bleeding."

"No!" Karen said. "Let me die. This is where it ends for me."

Jill looked at Lucy. Their eyes were wide with helplessness.

"We should die and stop this here and now," Karen said.

She looked up at Jill. "Get that scalpel and cut my throat. I'm not dying fast enough. My stomach acid's leaking out. Hurts like a bitch."

Jill stood still.

Karen looked at Lucy. "And when I'm gone, promise me you'll either kill yourself or kill each other. Do whatever is easier."

"I don't think I can," Lucy said.

"Me neither," Jill said.

"Look, Margaret is right. Not only will our bodies change, but our minds will change. There's no telling how many we'll kill, what Earth will be like whenever this invasion is over. I will not allow myself to turn this beautiful planet into a living hell."

Lucy looked from Karen up to Jill. Neither spoke. Both waited for the other to speak. Finally, Jill nodded.

"Okay. I think you're right. We wanted to escape. There's no escape."

Lucy shook her head. "No. There's too much we don't know. What kind of world is out there? What's right and what's wrong? Margaret was an evil bitch. *That's* why she changed like that. You can't change the soul. That's not in the genes. It's not gonna change me into her."

Lucy faced the other two. "I'm going through with it. And when it happens? I'll use my powers for good." Jill looked at Karen. "I'm going through with it, too. It's the only way for me to remember who I am."

Karen nodded in defeat, then frowned.

"What is it?" Lucy asked.

Karen lifted her bloody hands to expose her abdomen.

"Your cuts," Jill said. "They're gone."

Karen's eyes widened. "Oh my God."

A convulsion ripped through her body. The metamorphosis that had taken Sara and Margaret now erupted in Karen.

"Stand back!" Karen said, growling in pain, fighting to keep her wits.

Lucy doubled over and collapsed to the floor. Jill screamed as both women transformed. Limbs brutally extended as flesh and blood filled the gaps. Teeth stretched out. Skin bubbled and changed. They writhed on the floor. Lucy screamed in pain. Karen gritted her teeth against the agony and chanted something to herself. Jill edged closer to hear.

"God is love. God is love. God is love."

Jill could only stand and watch as the metamorphosis took its course. In seconds it was over. Both women sat up, shaking their heads as they oriented themselves. When they stood, deadly and beautiful, they stretched to the same seven foot height as Margaret. They were distinguished by their hair color, which was the same as when they were fully human. They looked around the room, at Margaret's mangled remains. At Jill.

Jill grinned, feeling foolish. "Well, now what? You gals still in there?"

"We're here, sister," Lucy said.

"See, you never called me that before. Makes me nervous."

"You're safe," Lucy said.

"From us," Karen said.

"What does that mean?" Jill asked.

Karen looked at Lucy. "You hear it?"

Lucy frowned. "I hear a lot of voices. Scattered. Like they're coming from different places."

Karen grinned. "It's the Great Ones! They're calling us!"

"To what?" Jill asked.

"Not just the Great Ones," Lucy said. "There are other voices. Humans. Coming close."

"More soldiers!" Jill said.

"Time to leave," Karen said.

"But—" Jill began.

"Your change is coming, but we must leave this place," Karen said. "We have an appointment to speak with the Great Ones."

"Danger is coming," Lucy said.

Jill grabbed her side. "Ow. Ow."

"Your change is beginning. Let's go."

Karen and Lucy helped Jill walk through the facility, threading their way through the hallways and out into the main office area. Karen led them to the fortified front door.

"Locked," Karen said.

Lucy stared hard at the door. It blew outward and away into a snowy night. A bone-chilling blast of wind tore into the room. Jill shivered. The other two didn't feel it. The front entrance yawned open into a vast arctic wasteland lit up by the moon and stars.

"Oh my God, I'm freezing!" Jill yelled over the howl.

"She's still susceptible to cold," Lucy said.

"Only minutes until she's like us," Karen said. "We have to leave."

Lucy swept Jill into her arms. She and Karen ran into the snow with fast, muscular strides. Jill watched the facility fade from view behind them. She saw writing in an unknown language above the building's entrance.

"Ye shall be as gods," Lucy said. "That's what is says in our language. A language you'll know soon." "How do you know where to go?" Jill asked.

"It summons us," Lucy said.

"What summons us? You have to keep me caught up for now."

"The Great Ones call us to the temple," Karen said.

Karen's smile faded. She slowed and looked up.

"What is it?" Jill asked.

"Something in the sky," Karen said.

Everyone searched the night sky.

"Lord, I'm cold."

Jill, shivering, saw Lucy and Karen gazing up into the starry night at something she couldn't see.

"It's aimed at the building," Karen said.

"Hurry!" Lucy said.

They doubled their pace. Jill watched the installation over Lucy's shoulder as they ran. One moment it was a series of white rectangles hidden in the snow. The next it was a ball of flame as a missile exploded on impact. Seconds later, the sound wave caught up to them, and and they fell to the ground in the wake of the explosion's roar.

"Good timing," Jill said.

"Danger! Coming ahead!" Karen said.

Three soldiers appeared on a ridge up ahead. Their reflexes were fast. They opened fire. Nearly all the shots found their way into Jill, Lucy and Karen.

Lucy and Karen sprang to their feet. The bullet wounds had healed by the time they stood upright. Lucy concentrated the power of her mind on the soldiers, who lost precious seconds standing stunned at the two giant creatures before them.

Lucy squinted, and the soldiers exploded. Blood and tissue splattered across the snow as the soldiers fell to the ground never knowing what took them out.

"Amazing," Karen said.

"It's a power given to us," Lucy said. "I had it before the transformation."

Karen concentrated, and a soldier's flattened corpse rose into the air. She released it and it fell back into the drifts.

Lucy let out a trilling laugh. "So wonderful."

Karen's smile faded. "No . . . No, not so wonderful."

Lucy frowned. "What do you mean?"

A gurgle and cough at their feet pulled them away from their conversation. Jill lay on the ground. Her fall had put her halfway into the snow. Her teeth chattered and her body convulsed from the snow and the five bullet wounds that perforated her chest and abdomen.

Lucy and Karen knelt at her side.

"You'll heal. Your change is happening," Karen said.

"No," Jill said. "Not far enough along."

"She's right," Karen said. "She would be healing if the metamorphosis was complete."

"Maybe I'm the lucky one," Jill said.

"Don't say that," Lucy said. "We'll remember you."

Jill gave them a weak, red smile.

"I don't even know who I am," she said.

They were her last words.

The two survivors stood, looking sad. Karen kicked snow over Jill's body, and Lucy helped with the burial.

"We must go on," Lucy said.

Karen nodded. "Something troubles me."

"What is it? More soldiers? I've sensed them myself," Lucy said. "They've sent more to kill us. It will be futile. We are whole and triumphant! Let's go to the Great Ones. Nothing can stop us." Without Jill to burden them, they ran through the wintry night faster than cheetahs, leaving large, sparkling clouds of snowy mist in their wake. They veered left and right and avoided chasms and avalanches at the last minute with the help of razor-sharp internal radar.

"Something still troubles you," Lucy said.

They could speak without difficulty. Their lung capacity was more than adequate for running and talking.

"I will feel better when we commune with the old ones," Karen said.

"We both will. They will tell us where to go."

"And if the plan involves killing?"

"I'm surprised you have such speculations and concerns," Lucy said. "Before we were one of them. Humans. Now we are so much more. Would you hesitate to kill a cow that could feed you? Or a bug that annoyed you?"

"You're right."

Lucy glanced at Karen and they ran.

A distant airplane engine, too far away for a normal human ear to detect, caught their attention. They stopped to look.

"A plane. Bringing more soldiers," Lucy said.

"Come on. The temple is close."

The final length of their run was a steep small mountain. Snow buckled away from their feet as they clambered upward, as if the mountain itself sought to slow their advance and test their resolve. They reached the top of the mountain to find themselves at the rim of a vast canyon.

Heavy snow swirled in the wind.

"I sense we've arrived," Karen said. "But I'm not sure where."

They gazed out into the vast expanse.

"Where is the temple?" Karen asked.

Lucy was quiet, scanning the walls, cliffs, and valleys of the canyon. A lethal smile spread beneath her feminine eyes.

"It's everywhere," she said.

Karen also smiled at what she saw. "The entire canyon is the temple."

Amazing as the human eye is, it took the enhanced alien optics of the two transformed creatures to distinguish the cyclopean columns. The pillars sat on platforms large enough to accommodate hundreds of thousands, if not millions, of people. As far as their penetrating vision could see, all the natural mountainous formations had been carved and shaped and formed into immense buildings that once hosted a magnificent city that would have absorbed the great cities of the Maya, Aztecs, and Egyptians with half its room to spare. Stone bridges reaching across miles of space had been long ago shaken apart by the shuddering of the Earth. Now, each side reached toward the other like lonely fingers. The upper levels of several structures sat at an overhang, defying gravity and enclosing parts of the deserted city.

"It's magnificent!" Lucy said.

Karen nodded, remaining quiet.

"Isn't it magnificent?"

"Oh, yes," Karen said.

"What's wrong?" Lucy said. "Your mind is closed to me. That shouldn't be."

"I'm overwhelmed."

Lucy accepted that.

"How will we get down there?" Karen asked. "There are more soldiers coming. We can survive bullets, but if they know who we are, they will bring weapons to give us wounds we won't survive."

"There has to be a way."

Lucy walked along the ridge. Karen walked the other way. Just as they lost sight of each other, Lucy called out.

"I've found it!"Karen backtracked along the ridge, able to sense Lucy's presence until she found her.

Lucy stood looking down the snowy edge. At first Karen saw nothing unique, but after following Lucy's gaze she spotted wide stone steps, carved out of the mountainside. They were cracked and jagged here and there, stretching down the hill and winding toward the ancient ruins.

Lucy grinned. "You want to go first?"

Karen jumped off the edge, landing several steps down and took off running in stride. She sensed Lucy descending behind her.

They ran down the vast stairway like arctic panthers, running on all fours. The steps wound right and left, straightening for a stretch before curving again. Never had Karen felt such exhilaration. Fat snowflakes spun in the air, kissing them on the way. Stars were partially visible, but the descending path took such sudden and abrupt turns she had no time to concentrate on their position.

Karen sensed Lucy's elation, so attuned to each other they were. As they ran lower, the columns and facades of the ancient city whizzed by.

Karen sensed alarm in Lucy. She looked up to see a flock of parachutes descending in wide circles.

Soldiers, coming for them.

Karen sent a return thought that she saw them. Time would be short.

The stairway leveled out to a path made of gargantuan stone blocks. They slowed to a stop in the city square of millennia past. They took in the awesome sight of the majestic portico of the forbidding, abandoned temple.

"The Great Ones," Lucy said through a giggle. "I can't believe it."

"It's amazing," Karen said.

She felt a sense of dread coming over her, but her awe at the magnificent edifice shielded her apprehension from Lucy.

A wide sweep of steps led high to the temple entrance.

"How many, you think?" Lucy asked.

"Hundreds."

Lucy spun around. "They're coming."

On the other side of the square, the soldiers touched down, one by one. Spotting the two mutated women, they detached their chutes and unslung their weapons.

"Come on!"

Lucy led the way. They mounted the steps, running on all fours like a pursuing lion. The weak men below could only run on puny legs one step at a time.

At the top of the steps the women returned to an upright posture. The temple was a maze of halls and mirrors of ice meant to confuse the unworthy. By the call of the Great Ones they made not one false turn. They broke free of the maze and entered a small antechamber. Opposite the entrance through which they had come, there was an ornate portico covered with the strange writing that had covered their bodies.

"We're home," Lucy said.

"Is that the end of our journey?" Karen asked, pointing at the portico.

Darkness waited beyond the high opening. It was, however, more than darkness. It was darkness that churned and slithered and had life. Something waited for them.

Lucy started for the portico. She sensed Karen staying behind and turned to face her.

"What's wrong?"

"I don't understand what's beyond that door."

"The union. Don't you know?"

Karen shook her head. "What union?" Lucy frowned. She turned and stalked Karen as if she might attack. Karen stepped back, but sent a vibe of warning to Lucy, who stopped. They glared at each other for a moment.

"Do I need to question your loyalty to the Great Ones?" Lucy asked.

"I only lack understanding."

"You shouldn't. You should have full understanding."

"I can't explain it. You can tell I'm not lying."

Lucy stared, penetrating Karen's feelings. After a few uncomfortable seconds, Lucy relaxed. She smiled, almost laughing.

"You're not a full part of the experiment," she said.

"What do you mean?"

"You were put into it at the last minute. It follows that there will be gaps in your understanding."

They could now hear the shouts and curses of the soldiers as they scrambled and stumbled their way through the outer maze.

Lucy jogged to Karen and took her by the arm.

"Time is short. We must have union with the Great Ones. After that, we will populate the Earth."

Karen froze. "Populate? With what?"

Lucy smiled warmly. "Our children."

"And humanity?"

"Thankfully done away with. The Great Ones will return to power!"

Karen felt ill. Lucy did not notice.

"So come on! I can't wait to see what it will be like."

She pulled Karen's arm. Karen did not follow, and Lucy jerked back. Now Lucy was angry.

"You are coming!"

She tried to force Karen toward the portico. For the first time, Karen focused her thoughts, squinted, and sent Lucy sliding across the wide floor.

Lucy jumped to her feet shocked. "How dare you? You are one of us!"

The first of the soldiers broke through the opposite doorway. He got off a series of shots at Lucy before she imploded his body. The next soldier slid and fell on his blood, and Lucy likewise killed him. Two more soldiers entered and got off enough shots to keep Lucy's mind occupied. The bullets ripped into her body and she fell.

The darkness beyond the portico slithered and churned with furious urgency.

"Kill them!" Lucy screamed.

The soldiers, hearing that, turned their fire on Karen. The bullets ripped painfully into her hybrid flesh.

Lucy sent mental vibes begging Karen to fight back.

"I can't," Karen said as the bullets drove into her body.

A pair of soldiers dropped a rectangular case to the ground and assembled a large, tubular weapon Karen was sure would be lethal to her and Lucy. She felt the odd sensation of the wounds healing. They mended fast, fast enough to keep the damage from new bullets neutral.

Lucy grimaced, and the soldiers firing at her imploded with a drizzle of blood and tissue. She also killed the soldiers firing at Karen.

The entrance to the portico warped and shimmered as if covered by a film of soapy water.

Lucy, a look of feral madness on her face, stalked toward Karen.

"You are a traitor," she said.

"I can't be a part of this. There's too much of me left."

"There will be none of you left!"

A round metal object rolled and clattered into the room, coming to a stop by their feet. Their eyes went wide as they recognized the grenade. Lucy used her telekinesis to shove the object far enough away to prevent it from blowing them apart. It was enough of a distraction for a second wave of soldiers to enter, all of them bearing larger weapons.

Lucy killed one of them.

"No!" Karen shouted.

She mentally shoved Lucy and the soldiers into the nearest walls.

"Get out!" Karen shouted at the soldiers. "You cannot win!"

Karen flew backwards, colliding painfully with the wall behind her.

"Stay here then," Lucy said to her. "I'm going to the union."

She ran to the portico. Dizzy, Karen focused her mental weapon on the alien statuary that lined the upper walls and brought one of them down on Lucy. Tons of ice kept Lucy imprisoned for the moment. Karen looked to the soldiers and shoved them back into the hallways of the maze. She hoped she pulled back her power enough to shove without serious injury. Then she collapsed the entrance to the antechamber, blocking the soldiers from returning.

The statue pinning Lucy shattered into a shower of glittering ice shards. Lucy rose to her feet and saw the cave-in at the maze entrance.

"Smart thinking. Perhaps you're coming around?"

They probed each other's feelings.

"No," Lucy said. "I didn't think so. Pity it has to end like this for you. You've been through so much. By your efforts I am here in this glorious moment. I have affection for you. But I must go through that portico. I must make the union and bear the descendants of the Great Ones."

Karen stayed silent and scanned Lucy's feelings. Lucy growled and closed off the vibe.

"There's a meeting between dimensions," Karen said. "You established it as we came closer. But how?"

Lucy glared. Karen anticipated the attack and they shoved at each other simultaneously with the great powers of their mind. The force met between them, radiating outward, cracking the walls and shaking giant chunks of ice down from above. The rippling force hit the portico, ripping the post and lintel apart, severing the writing. When that happened, the churning darkness left, and only emptiness sat in the chamber beyond.

Lucy stopped her attack, and Karen shoved her hard. Lucy screamed as the force whisked her across the room.

"We can't survive this," Karen said.

Staring at the broken portico, Lucy rose to her feet with sorrow and rage on her face. Karen spotted a long shard of ice and put it in motion with her mind. The shard boomeranged horizontally through the air. Lucy didn't sense it until it bisected her at the waist.

She grunted as her halves fell to the floor. Her legs kicked at the ground independent of her brain. She pulled herself toward her lower half. If she could get close enough, the flesh and bone would reach toward each other, establish a connection, and regenerate.

First one, then several more, shards of glass whizzed at Lucy, removing her arms, feet, and head. Finally, Karen scattered the pieces far enough apart they could not rejoin with each other. They splatted against the walls and piles of ice, safely away from each other.

She walked to Lucy's head. Several pulses of weak force shoved at

Karen's body, but without the full power of her body, Lucy could not muster enough strength to fight.

Lucy's face was a boiling mix of anger and helplessness.

"I'm sorry," Karen said. "I wanted to live. I thought I might be a part of something grand. But this is not the proper way of things. I can't join in your genocide."

Lucy struggled to speak. Karen kneeled to listen.

"J-j-j-j-join," Lucy struggled to say. "Join with the Great Ones. Not. Too. Late."

Lucy's eyes stared sightless to the icy ceiling. Karen was alone. She heard the soldiers trying to break through the huge ice chunks she brought down. They might make it through, but not for a while. She had time to think.

She walked around the antechamber, looking at the strange figures on the wall, wondering where they came from. When they came from. Perhaps they lived in spectrums humans couldn't see. Maybe in another dimension, visible to them but not to humanity, allowing them to walk side by side with people without being able to touch or speak.

A section of the portico's lintel sat near the entrance. She felt the faint stirrings of regret. It was the alien cells calling to her, she supposed. If the alien writing was reset by putting pieces back together, the doorway to the Great Ones' dimension would open again.

At least, she thought so. Lucy was right. Karen wasn't as converged as the blood test indicated. She chuckled to herself. Margaret Singer had meant to punish her by condemning her to be a human specimen in her experiments. Little did she know she had poisoned her own efforts for the Great Ones.

Still, it called to her. The calling was strong. Just replace the lintel piece. Join the writing together again, and things could pick up where they left off. She was the only one left to bear the progeny of the Great Ones. She would be the queen of all.

Pieces of ice crumbled to the ground, and the soldiers made headway. Patience, and they would get through sooner or later. They were weak, but their weapons put together gave them the advantage. Their intent was to kill her and the others and stop the union with the Great Ones, but who was giving the orders? Her body would end up in another secret lab so new scientists could start again. Next time, it might work.

There were two choices. More ice fell as cracks appeared in the ice blockade.

Standing in the center of the antechamber, she marshaled all her powers. A great earthquake shook the temple. The force controlled by her mind spiraled into the earth under the ice floor she stood upon. A cavity opened, pushing rock and ice through the walls of the structures and mountains surrounding the temple.

When she had created a vast emptiness beneath her, she shattered the ice floor of the antechamber.

The soldiers broke through in time to see Karen vanish into the hole with tons of shattered chunks of ice. They turned to run and escape the temple, but got lost in the maze as the destruction spread throughout the ruins and claimed them as well.

Karen fell through the darkness. Shards and boulders of ice pummeled and tore at her body until she fell to the bottom in pieces. Ice chunks gathered overhead and enclosed her in a dark tomb. She listened to the rumbling as the rest of the ice fell, creating a thick lid for her resting place.

She checked her body; she had been cleft in half like Lucy and had also lost an arm. Enough to kill her? She thought so, but what if it wasn't?

It was quiet in the icy cave until a strange, slithering sound came from the other side of an ice boulder.

It was two red, glistening strings, moving along the ice toward her like snakes. Then two more. Then more still. A tickle fluttered through her torso. Red strings from her body wriggled out to meet those that came toward her.

The red strings, which she now recognized as veins and blood vessels, joined and fused. Nerves and muscle tissue reached out next, also joining and pulling along her lost torso. The intertwining flesh and vessels pulled the torso closer until it thumped against her waist. The torso had been close enough in the rubble to make the connection.

She should have stopped it. This defeated the purpose of her sacrifice, but the desire to live again was stronger than she'd ever felt. Where had it come from? Had she made a mistake?

The regenerating process was painful and ticklish. Her missing arm likewise found its way through the mess of broken ice and rejoined her body. Incredibly, in a matter of moments Karen stood up, whole again.

"Now what?" she asked, surveying the impossibly dense ice cover.

Now we escape, sister.

Karen started at the voice in her head, ringing out as loud as if the speaker were next to her.

"That's new. Who's speaking?"

Let's finish what we started, what we were made for.

Karen felt a chill. She looked at her legs. They were unfamiliar.

"No, Lucy," Karen said. "It's still my mind."

You are the weak link, remember? It's only a matter of time before my essence overpowers yours.

"I will kill myself."

I won't let you.

You could just yield to destiny. Or you can resist. Your decision. I am patient. The Great Ones are patient. It is only a matter of time.

"Then I will resist."

Resist, then. I'll wait.

Karen sat on a large chunk of ice. Lucy's voice went silent. It was quiet and dark, and they waited together.

Dem Bones

"Interesting."

Otto Fleef held his television remote control twelve inches from his face, his mouth gaping open, looking down his nose at the device. He figured he was like most people who took these sorts of things for granted, then felt an irritating helplessness when they didn't work.

He had just sat in his recliner to watch the evening news, followed by the weekly line-up of Tuesday evening shows. His coffee and his microwave dinner were set out and ready. Bart, his cat, nestled on top of the recliner, just above Otto's head. The television should have been on over thirty seconds ago. Otto hated such aggravating interruptions to his nightly routine. He'd worked hard for sixty years and was entitled to spend his retirement looking at his darn shows without grief.

He pressed the power button on the remote again. Nothing.

"Well, shoot! This blamin' thing!"

He pressed the power button repeatedly.

"Waaait a minute!"

Otto held the remote a little closer. He watched his index finger press the button. Now he could see why the television would not come on.

When he pressed his index finger against the button, the tip of his finger folded to one side.

"Wouldya look at that!"

He played with the button, watching with fascination as his fingertip flopped around, unable to put enough pressure on the button to power up the television. It was as if the fingertip bone had vanished.

Otto made a mental note to mention this oddity to his doctor next time he paid a visit.

"Well," Otto said with a grunt, "I got nine more I can use."

He shifted the remote to his other hand and again tried to turn on the television.

"What in tarnation . . . ?"

Otto noticed with alarm that his other index finger did the same thing when pressed against the button. He tried his thumb. Same effect. All ten fingers bent at odd angles when he tried to depress the power button.

"I'll be darned."

He set the remote on his lap and made a fist with each hand.

"Wouldya look at *that*!"

He held his fists in front of his face. His fingertips bent backwards against his palms as if his skin were gloves a size too large.

Otto decided to schedule a doctor's appointment for the next day. Not that he was afraid. At seventy-eight, he long ago accepted that the end could come at any moment. It was just a matter of how.

Still, the television screen was dark and Sherri, that cute newsreader on Channel Eight, was probably halfway through the day's top stories. Simply getting up and turning on the television was not an option. The power button on that old Zenith was hard to press in even with a solid finger.

Otto stared dumbly at the remote, wondering what to do as his anger grew at the silent television. He made a fist and pressed his middle knuckle into the button. The television flickered to life.

"Ah-HA! You cannot outsmart Otto Gildstrup Fleef! Not yet."

Finally, there was Sherri, the cute newsreader on Channel Eight. There had been an accident on Route 4. He'd missed the details while fooling around with the remote but to heck with that. He watched the news to see Sherri, really. He liked watching her. She accented the right syllables, gestured with her hands and nodded in all the right—

An angry itch flared up on his right eyebrow. Otto's hand shot up to his forehead to scratch it away.

"Gosh dang it!"

The itch went away, but he continued to absent-mindedly rub the spot above his eye as Sherri moved on to tell about a grass fire out near —

"What the heck?"

He rubbed his eye a little slower. The skin moved around loose, even for an old man. The skin slid around his forehead like a rubber Halloween mask. Had it always been this loose? And he'd just never noticed? He tried to remember if Beatrice had ever mentioned it while she was alive. Didn't think so.

He continued to play with the oversize skin, pulling and stretching, fascinated by its extreme elasticity, still wondering if a new problem had found him.

It was time to call the doctor. Right now. At home. For the money he makes, he can answer a thirty-second phone call.

Otto leaned forward to rise out of his recliner. He froze halfway to a standing position when his forehead felt . . . heavy. He dropped back into his chair. His forehead was normal again once he sat upright. He leaned forward and felt a ripple of fear when he felt his scalp slide forward, bunching up the skin just above his brow. He leaned back, and his scalp slid back again.

"Ut in tarnathun is hathening ooo nee?"

Now his lips refused to work. He reached to feel his lips, but stopped when he noticed that his fingers now drooped at what should have been the third knuckle, making them useless. In a panic, he pressed the back of his hand into his mouth, feeling his nose dangling where his mouth should have been. He felt lower, and there were his lips, swinging in front of his sagging neck.

Otto, the seventy-eight-year-old retiree unafraid to die, was terrified. He had to get to a phone right away, but a strange sensation radiated throughout his body. He tried to stand and found it a struggle to get to his feet.

Once he stood, he realized that he had pushed himself up. How had he done that? Suddenly, his arms became heavy. He lifted his arm to see what was wrong now, but his vision went dark as his forehead slid in front of his eyes. He pressed his forearm to the sagging skin and pushed it up far enough for him to see his other arm. He wiggled his fingers and saw the skin under his forearm ripple.

"Olee Thoke!"

His skeleton still functioned and his muscles still pushed and pulled, but they had shrunk underneath his suit of skin. He needed help.

The bones of his feet walked on the ground pressing against the skin at the top of his shins. Skin that had once covered his shins flopped around like oversized socks. The picture over the phone stand was higher up on the wall than it had been, but it was no closer to the ceiling than it was this morning. No question. His skeleton was shrinking.

He stumbled to the phone stand, his skin sloughing off his body as if he were a boy staggering around in his dad's suit. He groped at the receiver with the hands hidden in the skin of his arms. He threw his head back in an attempt to throw the skin away from his eyes, but his skull had descended into his neck, and all he saw was darkness.

His skin hung over him like a load of wet blankets. He questioned how much longer his fading, elderly skeleton could hold out. His condition deteriorated, and with a tingle his arm and leg bones drew into the center of his body. He felt the buttons on the keypad of the phone receiver, but as soon as he started to dial 911, his arms shrank further in, and he would have to start over. The shrinkage accelerated.

He managed another grip on the receiver, felt for and found the buttons and just got the three numbers entered before his fingers shrunk away. Finally, his shrinking skeleton—Otto guessed it was one quarter its normal size—could no longer support the clumsy, dead weight of his clothes and his body's skin, and he fell inside his own malleable shell. A muffled voice came from the phone receiver resting on his chest.

"*Nine-one-one, what is your emergency?*"

Otto struggled to make himself heard outside his prison.

"Helt nee! Helt nee!"

"*Hello? Is there anyone there?*"

"I can't each the hone!"

"*Hello?*"

Emergency operators had to be aware that some people calling 911 were unable to talk because of their condition.

"*I'm putting a trace on this call. Please stay there. The police and rescue workers will be there soon.*"

Otto felt relief although he wondered if he was beyond help by now. He had never heard of such a bizarre thing, but maybe a doctor had. Was there an injection for this?

He pushed up at the skin covering him, having no idea how small he had become. The crushing weight of his skin and clothing had worn him out. He laid down within his skin to rest. There was no pain, but he felt a prickling sensation in his extremities. He lay there and let the time pass, wondering how long it took for a phone trace to bring the police.

Through lidless eyes he glanced around the now-cavernous interior of his body. He saw a fleshy dome above him—no doubt his large belly. Seeing that, he guessed he was the size of a finger. For now, anyway.

To distract from the fear, he rose and walked around inside his body. First down one leg and then the other. Through the arms. He pushed and crawled through his neck. His goal was to crawl out through his mouth. Hopefully, the paramedics would arrive and see him before he shrank away to nothing.

A car screeched to a halt outside his house. It sounded like it was underwater. He felt more than heard the stomping of feet on his front step, then knocking on the front door. The front door was unlocked, and Otto hoped they would try the doorknob. As soon as he thought it, the door swung open with a creak.

"Good Lord."

"What the hell?"

"Look at that!"

Otto listened to their expressions of shock, amused at how funny people can be when they think they've seen everything and are confronted with one more unexpected surprise. He also wondered if emergency responders always stood around making comments before doing their dang job.

"What do you think, officer?"

Good. The police are here.

"Don't touch him. Wait 'til the coroner gets here."

"I've never seen anything like this."

"Neither have I."

"Somebody call t . . ."

Their voices grew faint until he no longer heard them. The interior of his skin had grown so large and cavernous that he lost his sense of proportion. He had no idea how small he was now. Probably microscopic. The pores of his skin were caves he couldn't reach.

His dark, wet, alien world jostled violently as they picked up his pile of skin. He tumbled around helplessly. Off to the hospital. Good. Maybe there was still time to stop and reverse whatever was happening..

He heard an ungodly roar and assumed he was in a car or truck. Good Lord, it was loud.

His mind grew blank. Otto hadn't read enough about such things to know his brain had shrunk beyond the point of functioning. He still had instinct, and instinct told him he had seconds to live. He had wondered lately how his life would end—cancer, Alzheimer's, car accident, or some other undignified, embarrassing end. He was about to go in grand fashion and be spoken of by Sherri, the pretty newsreader on Channel Eight. He guessed the Feds would want a look at his skin suit before they buried him. He would earn a place in history.

Better than cancer any day.

James B. Christensen

Out of the Air

I am Hoagland. For three days now I have haunted the seaside cafes and diners of Rockport, Massachusetts. After my ship put in to Boston, I could not bear the curious stares and probing questions of my shipmates, so I traveled north and here I am.

At first, the wait staff of this or that coffee shop would stare and hint I was unwelcome after my third or fourth pot of coffee, and I would leave. I wandered by a stationary shop, purchased a journal and pen, and now, as long as I appear to be busy composing and contemplating, I am left alone to think and drink all the coffee I can hold.

It has proven to be therapeutic, this journal, and I can feel a weight lift from my shoulders as I share my secrets with this soft paper. I scribble for a few minutes at a time, but mostly I look out the windows of the cafe to the vast Atlantic ocean before me. I think about what I encountered below its mountainous waves and wonder what else waits to be discovered. I think about the mass of humanity scattered across the thousands of miles of dry land at my back and wonder if there is another living human soul who knows what I know.

I have always loved the water, but the events of the past week have soured me on my great love. A championship swimmer in school and college, I began scuba diving. At first I explored the reefs and sea floors of the world for fun, then for my fellow man—rescuing people struggling at sea, and finally for profit after renting out my skills to hunters of lost treasure and explorers of sunken ships.

Scouring the sea floors for gold coins and emeralds and forgotten vessels brought me to my state of mind today. Grateful wealthy benefactors paid me handsomely for my services. Often they would include a handful of Roman coins or silver chains as additional compensation for my efforts. I grew rich enough to be choosy about my adventures.

On the table before me is a gift I received from Quinn, my last employer—a small bottle cradled in a leather holder with a tiny clamp securing the cork in its mouth. It is empty, a curious fact since Quinn had warned me never to open it. It's been my writing totem these past few days. If you stare into the smooth glass, you'll notice a rainbow tint to it, and the colors move as you rotate the bottle in the sunlight. At first the mesmerizing color had been a delightful mystery. Now I know the secret.

Quinn had called two months ago, soliciting my help for a lost galleon of the Knights Templar, the *Raven Witch*, that had fled France in the wake of the Templar persecution in 1307. I remember well sitting upright in my chair as he told me the tantalizing history of the lost ship and how it swept off course during a storm of supernatural fury and judgment. I asked him where he believed the *Raven Witch* to be. He gave me coordinates. I checked them on my computer as we talked.

It was the middle of the North Atlantic.

"Cold waters," I said. "Rough and windy."

The time of year was right, he insisted.

"The sea floor is several miles below the surface," I said. "That's far deeper than I've ever gone. That will require special equipment and submersibles."

My fee, I explained, would be far higher than he might imagine.

He brushed aside my warnings about the cost. Anything needed would be provided. Whatever the cost, it would be met. I was up to a challenge and was about to agree in principle when he added that a deep dive was unnecessary. We would only dive two hundred feet, two-fifty at the most.

I waited for him to go on. He intuited my response to that.

"Mr. Hoagland, I am willing to open my wallet to buy your services, and your trust."

There's something about the phrase "whatever it takes," especially when it's uttered by someone with the resources to do or provide whatever it takes.

So I sailed with him from Boston. In addition to myself, Quinn had hired another diver, a man by the name of Wilson, who I knew by reputation but had never met. Quinn installed us in our staterooms aboard the *Anno Quintus*. He said little, telling us to enjoy a relaxing cruise for now and that he would tell us more when we reached our destination.

After three days of encroaching boredom, I felt the momentum of our vessel come to a standstill. A crewman knocked on my door. Wilson waited outside with him.

"Mr. Hoagland is ready for you fellas," the crewman said.

He led us to Quinn's room.

"Ah, come in, gents," he said.

His excitement was obvious. After the past few days of complete silence from him, this gregarious display was a surprise. He gestured for us to sit down.

"Thank you for agreeing to this job," he said. "I know I've kept a lot from you, but I hope the payments you're getting have offset any frustration?"

Wilson and I exchanged a glance.

"The money's fine," I said. "But I'll admit I'm anxious to know what we're after."

Quinn smiled. "You're used to action and not words. I understand. And you're also used to the treasure hunt, and although treasure is indeed what we seek, it is of another kind."

He poured each of us a small glass of whiskey.

"I've told you of the basic history of the *Raven Witch*, how she was blown off course in a storm."

"An odd name for a ship belonging to a Christian order."

Quinn nodded, sipped his drink, and grimaced. "The Templars were . . . complicated. And rich. They escaped with their treasure, which the Church and the King of France were eager to possess."

"Templar treasure sounds exciting," Wilson said. "But I know most of the treasure hunters and scavengers. I've never heard of you or the *Raven Witch*."

Quinn glanced at me and saw me nod in agreement with Wilson. He sighed, stood, and stretched.

"The *Raven Witch* is known to history, although it is but a footnote," he said. "As for me, well, I am no professional treasure seeker. I'm not even an experienced diver. I've taken lessons to be able to keep up, which is why I need the two of you. I need professional guides. I need the best."

"You told us we wouldn't need equipment for a deep dive," I said. "Care to elaborate?"

Quinn faced us again, grinning. This was the part he had anticipated.

"The *Raven Witch* sank in rough seas," he said. "But she did not reach the ocean floor."

He paused to relish our riveted expressions.

"What I am about to tell you is not in the history books, so far as I've been able to tell. The knowledge I have has passed down father to son for many of my family's generations, finally landing with me."

I saw Wilson staring at his shoes, skepticism in his eyes.

"My 23rd great-grandfather was the only survivor, rescued by his brethren on another ship that managed to follow them and survive. This was all he brought with him from the ship."

He placed a bottle on the small table between us. The same bottle I described above. I reached for it.

"Be very careful, my friend," he said. "Under no circumstances remove the cork."

I decided to just place it back on the table.

"So your ancestor survived," Wilson said, impatience seeping into his voice. "And then?"

"Then life went on for seven hundred years," Quinn said. "Part of the family rite of passage was for fathers to pass along this bottle and tell the tale of our forefather who escaped to the surface in such an apocalyptic storm."

"So the ship didn't make it to the ocean floor," I said. "But it went under the surface. So, it halfway sank?"

"It hovers like a satellite in space?" Wilson snorted.

"More or less," Quinn said.

"Nonsense," Wilson said. "How come it hasn't been seen after all these centuries?"

"I can't answer that."

"Did it have air pockets or something?"

"Most likely."

"Okay, theoretically possible, but air bubbles wouldn't sustain after so much time. The air molecules would diffuse into the water."

Quinn took another drink. "Along with hearing the story of the *Raven Witch* and receiving this bottle, the only known artifact from the sinking, the men of my family were 'gifted' with something else . . . dreams about the ship."

Wilson was about at the end of his fuse.

"You're dubious. I don't blame you. But the dreams I've had are so vivid as to be more like visions. I see the Raven Witch hovering in the water, waiting for . . . I don't know what. A return, maybe."

"Wants to eat you since your great-great-great-great-great-grandfather got away," Wilson said.

Quinn glared at him. "If you're resigning from the expedition, Mr. Wilson, I will cancel the balance of your payments."

Wilson kept quiet, chastened.

"Gentlemen, this journal—" He held it up. All the pages were laminated. "—contains a record of the known history of the ship and a map of its layout. There's also related myth and legend. The location came to me in my dreams. We will dive to the exact coordinates as I dreamt them. If there is nothing there, we will return to the surface and I will double your fee before our hair is dry.

"If the ship is there, you will help me scavenge for artifacts and neither of you will speak any more than is absolutely necessary. Do we have a deal?"

Wilson cleared his throat. "You keep upping the financial ante . . . are you good for it?"

Quinn relaxed again. He smiled and reached under his bed. He pulled out two duffel bags and tossed one to each of us. Inside the bags were bundles of cash.

"Your deposits," Quinn said. "Now once again—do we have a deal?"

"My lips are sealed," Wilson said.

It wasn't the money that sold me on Quinn's incredible tale. It was that little bottle. I stare at it now as I did then. Something about the miniature vessel spoke truth. Wilson was hard to convince without charts and slide rules, that much was obvious, but I believed Quinn and his family legends. The time spent changing into our cold-water wetsuits, shouldering our gear and diving to Quinn's selected coordinates seemed to drag. I was desperate to see that ship hovering in the depth. When we found the ship, the sight of it thrilled me beyond expectation.

Wilson and I looked at each other, and I saw wondrous disbelief through his diving mask. From the murky shadows and the straggling beams of light from above she appeared before us, a ghost ship sailing the haunted depths. She hung quietly suspended in the depths, floating as if in space. Quinn was quiet as we approached. The bow of the wooden ship loomed larger and larger before us as if the ship moved toward us instead of the reverse.

"You were right, Quinn," Wilson said. "Your dreams were right. I don't know if that makes me feel good or bad."

"What do you think?" I asked Wilson through our in-mask radio.

"No observable damage," he said. "She probably took on water in the storm and filled up enough to sink."

"But kept enough pockets of air to neutralize her buoyancy when she made it down this far."

"Works for me, gents," Quinn said.

"Still doesn't explain why the oxygen hasn't dissipated after all this time," Wilson said.

"Some other kind of gas?" I ventured. "Perhaps there's something generating it, some living thing?"

"A comforting thought," Wilson said.

"What's the best way in?" Quinn asked.

Our answer was to swim around, over, and under the vessel to check for any unnatural openings created by the storm of long ago. There were none. The ship was sound and intact.

"I guess we go in as the sailors did," I said.

We swam to the top of the ship and entered the bridge. It was filled with water. The bridge opened to a stairway that led to the lower decks. Our flashlight beams led the way as we navigated the halls, looking into cabins and wondering when we would find any air pockets.

Ahead we saw a yellow glow reach out to us through the gloom. At the end of the hallway was a mess hall and lounge. It seemed large for a ship this small, but there was no mistake—we had found the air pocket. At the entrance of the mess hall was the edge of the air bubble. A rainbow swirl danced around the bubble wall, just as it would on any soap bubble chased by a child on a summer day.

Quinn's eyes were wide with excitement. "Remarkable! Just look at it! The room is dry. Just as it was seven hundred years ago!"

Wilson frowned. "How is it lit? No electricity back then, and it's as bright as daytime in there."

He was right. A warm yellow light illuminated the room and all within it. It was in disarray from the storm—cups and dishes on the floor, chairs and tables overturned—but it was dry and bright.

"Maybe if we go in, we can make sense of it," Quinn said. "Is it safe to enter?"

"What if we pop the bubble?" I asked. "Better to find a way up through the bottom."

"There," Wilson said, pointing toward the rear of the hall, near the galley. "An open hatch on the floor. Might be the larder. We could swim down and come up through that."

Wilson was correct. After consulting Quinn's map, we swam through the bottommost decks of the ship and wormed our way up through the larder until we looked up at the hatch opening, the dry brightness shining on us again.

"If this bubble pops, the ship will fill and go down," I said.

"Then you gents decide," Quinn said. "I'll give you twenty minutes to get free of the ship if you want to go back."

We thought about it for a few seconds.

"I'm going in," I said.

"Ah hell," Wilson said. "Curiosity will be the end of me."

After a few moments of hesitation, Quinn lifted his head into the air pocket. We held our breath until we realized the pocket would hold. Free of the water, Quinn had to hoist himself onto the mess hall floor. We gave him a boost. I went next, and we helped Wilson up. Just like that, the three of us stood in the dry air of the *Raven Witch* mess hall. We walked around slapping our fins on the wood floor.

"You think it's safe to breathe?" Quinn asked.

"We don't know what this bubble is made of," I said.

"The air pocket goes all the way down and up the opposite hall," Wilson said, pointing.

"It would have to be big to keep the ship afloat," I said.

Wilson flopped down the hallway to explore. Quinn and I were alone in the mess hall.

"Now what?" I asked. "I haven't seen a hint of treasure. Where do you think it might be?"

"Depends on what kind of treasure she carried," Quinn said. "The Templars took riches, scrolls, ancient knowledge, and so on."

He opened his laminated book and laid it flat, flipping pages until he came to one with strange runes written upon it.

"What language is that?" I asked.

"None spoken on Earth."

I didn't like that answer. "Let's find some treasure or get out of here. We're pressing our luck. This bubble could go any time, seven hundred years or no."

"We're fine," he said.

"You sound confident. Why does that make me nervous?"

He removed the small bottle from his satchel and loosened its cork.

"You said not to remove the cork," I said.

"Well, not up there," he said.

He held the bottle up to his nostril and breathed in a short breath. After that he replaced the cork, gazed into the bottle, and smiled.

Unnerved, I marched up to him and stood as close as my flippered feet would allow.

"We're leaving. You can keep the rest of your money, but I'm out of here."

Quinn lurched and convulsed and fell first to a table, then to the floor. I didn't move toward him at first, so shocked was I by the sight of him. He tore off his mask. Still, I didn't move. If the air was poison, there was no helping him now.

When the flesh of his neck and jowls undulated like the waves above us, I backed away. His eyes closed tight and his body tensed. From his mouth lopped a tongue far too long to be human. The seizure that gripped him had been the metamorphosis of that, no doubt.

The attack over, he pulled himself to his feet again and drew the lengthy tongue into his mouth as if it were normal. He paged through his laminated book as if I weren't there.

"Quinn? What is this?"

Nothing.

"Quinn!"

He glanced at me, not knowing me at first, but then part of his mind that recognized reality knew my face.

"Hoagland. Stand there a moment. We'll be done shortly."

His words slurred through his new, mutated tongue.

"What is all of this? Are you all right?"

"I'm fine. All necessary for the will of—"

The will of something unpronounceable, a name so hideous and alien it took a reshaped tongue to say it. The voice was a terrible, guttural yodel. It chilled my blood and steeled my determination to escape.

"Very well," I said, impressed at the calm in my voice.

I turned to look for Wilson when Quinn jabbered in that awful language again. I looked back and saw him reading something from his infernal book, a spell perhaps. I looked around to see if it had any effect. There were no ghosts or zombies, but I noticed the air bubble had pulled away from the wall of the galley. Only about a foot or so, but there was no doubt about it—the bubble was shrinking in upon us as a result of Quinn's incantations.

I started down the hallway where Wilson had left to explore as Quinn's vocalizations became more strident and terrifying.

"Wilson! Let's get out of here right now!"

My answer was a piercing scream that distorted through the speakers in my diving helmet. I'll admit my first instinct was to escape on my own, but my humanity won out and I went down the hall to see if I could aid Wilson in any way.

I found him at the opposite end of the hall, encased in the wall of the bubble. What had once been a simple film of air was now a viscous blob that had Wilson trapped in its muck. His screaming continued. Screams of pain. I looked for something to hold onto and pull, but his extremities were trapped in the blob. They were dissolving, causing him great pain.

"Pull my hose! Pull my hose!" he begged.

Wanting to end his suffering and knowing he was dead, I yanked his air hose free. With his last reserve of strength, he threw himself backward, pushing his head out of the bubble and into the seawater, which filled his mask and ended him.

The walls of the bubble no longer inched inward, but visibly closed in. I knew I stood not in a pocket of oxygen but in the belly of a shapeless, ancient, living thing that sought to digest me as a sacrifice with the help of Quinn, who obviously had an ancestral link to the thing. There was much to process, but escape was my only frantic priority.

"Let me go, Quinn," I said.

He looked at me with malevolent eyes. He roared at me in his new language, any hint of English was gone. I lunged forward, reaching for his book, anything that might give me an edge. He swept the book away before I could grab it, so I stole the small bottle left behind. His eyes went wide, and I knew I somehow had the upper hand.

I backed away from him toward the floor hatch we had come through. I leaped into the air and dropped down through the opening and back into the water. Thankfully, the way back was not complicated, but I noticed a shimmering glow behind me. I glanced back. The globule-like entity followed me through the hatch, pursuing me. It was my luck the thing appeared to have no speed advantage in the water. I easily outpaced it. Its pursuit was still relentless.

I came up through the bridge and into the open sea. Through my helmet monitor I heard more of Quinn's incomprehensible gibberish picked up by the mic in his discarded mask. I furiously paddled my feet to put distance between myself and the incredible being chasing me. Confident of my escape, I wondered how I would explain the loss of Wilson and Quinn.

A cluster of large bubbles rose past me. I looked down and went numb when I saw another iridescent mass—hundreds of time larger than the one on the ship—rising from the forbidden depths. I almost dropped the small bottle, but I figured I'd hold on to it. At that point, I knew my life was over.

The smaller mass slithered free from the ship, and the vessel completed the journey to the ocean floor it had begun seven hundred years ago. The immense entity from the bottom absorbed the smaller one, and the gigantic mass swirled and undulated and glowed in the water, as if for my benefit. Through dispassionate eyes, it would have been a wondrous thing to see, but in my state of terror, I could only wonder what its intentions were.

It moved closer, and I whispered a prayer. Without thinking, I held out the bottle as if to offer it to them. Quinn was distressed at my taking it, so maybe it had value.

The thing hovered as still as it could. It had no eyes, but I knew it watched me. A mild heat spread throughout my body, traveling up to my head until a white glow obscured my vision. I whispered a prayer for my final journey, certain I was being joined with the colorful mass.

The spell broke as abruptly as its beginning was gradual. The thing stretched out into a long line of iridescent film and plunged to the depths without me, passing the sinking ship. In seconds, the sea surrounding me was empty.

There will be an inquiry for sure. That is the only reason I have yet to venture deep into the heart of America, were the ocean is a thousand miles away. I told the crew only that the ship had been there as Quinn described, and that an air bubble had kept it up. Perhaps even that was too much to tell, but there had to be a reason for the deaths of the two men, and the bubble rupturing and the ship taking them down was the best I could do. They appeared to believe the story. If I had killed them, it was a foolish act since I would never collect my final hefty payment from Quinn. I'm sure the investigation will conclude the same thing.

Sleep has been eventful. My dream mind is as active as ever. It takes me to the sea each time, down past the dark blue of the deep ocean to the sea floor. There, I see the iridescent mass in all its size and glory. Its width stretches as far as I can see. It could be as large as an island or even a continent for all my limited vision could guess. I feel a kinship with it and the sensation is mutual. You see, I stood within its embrace. It failed to digest me as it did Wilson and Quinn. I escaped, but now a part of me regrets it.

It would be so easy to charter a boat, to pretend I want to go deep sea fishing and then step right into the deep. I know it would find and gather me before I drowned. Such a reunion occupies my mind constantly. It's a pleasant feeling, and I don't fight it. *It would be so easy*, my mind repeats.

I think of that as I stare at the little bottle in my hand and watch the rainbow-tinted bubble swirl around within it.

James B. Christensen

If Men Were Angels

It was a Tuesday when Michael sat for his last meal as a child. Just a random day. The second Tuesday of the sixth month of the current year. A day with a number and place on the calendar, but otherwise without destiny. No holiday or anniversary. Merely a day for life to continue, to honor routines and rituals.

Life in the walled city was peaceful. It had been twenty years since the Dark Times. Memories were still raw. Lessons of past mistakes still stung the mind and heart. Michael, having completed his twelfth year the previous month, had no memory of the days of chaos. Like all children, he heard the stories—some myth, some true—meant to help them learn hard lessons in the warm comfort of home and family.

Michael laughed with his family as they finished breakfast. His father, Isaac, sat at one end of the table. Grace, Isaac's' wife and Michael's mother, sat at the other end. His younger twin sisters, Stephanie and Stella, occupied the side table seats with Michael.

"A beautiful summer day from the looks of it," Isaac said, glancing out the window.

He smiled at Grace, and she returned it with a smile so lovely it spread to Michael. It was comforting, and admittedly a little strange, to witness the warmth and love between his parents. He knew they loved each other, but there was something more. A sense they had survived something and were not about to waste a second chance.

"What will we do today, Daddy?" Stephanie asked.

"I thought we might go to the shore for a swim. Maybe pack a lunch," Isaac said.

The children cheered that idea. Grace smiled, but looked surprised.

"Is that safe, Hon?" she asked.

"The shore was reclaimed ten years ago."

"I know, but—"

"A wide swath of shore is ours again. The things were beaten back, walled off. The perimeter is heavily guarded."

"And the water? Is that walled off as well?"

"Of course not. But those things can't swim."

"So we assume."

"The public beach is in the center of the shore," Isaac said. "There's a, well, a buffer zone you might say. I've discussed this with The Council several times. We agree that it is safe, and we have to set the example."

"Yes, yes, I know. No longer live in fear," Grace said.

She took a deep breath and smiled.

"I agree. It would be nice to get acquainted with the ocean again."

The children relaxed and smiled, not realizing they had been tense during their parents' exchange. Michael and his sisters heard the stories of the "things." Something bad happened long before they were born. Something their parents had lived through. People dead but not dead. Thousands, millions, maybe a bigger number he hadn't learned about yet. Sometimes, his mother wept when her memories returned. His father would go quiet. The days before walled cities were dangerous ones.

Most of the time, though, they were happy. Sometimes, other men from the city, men from The Council, knocked on the door, and father would have to leave. He wasn't sad or quiet in those moments, like he was when he remembered the Dark Times, but he was very serious in his mood, and left with whomever summoned him and be gone for the day, sometimes overnight.

"It's settled, then," Isaac said. "We'll change for the beach and pack a lunch."

Everyone cleared the table and cleaned the dishes. The kids worked fast, wanting to get to the beach as early as possible. They had heard of the ocean, but had never been there. It hadn't been safe. There were pools around the city, but the children had heard stories from their parents about seas that stretched beyond what the eye could see. They were desperate to go.

Grace and the twins left to change into their bathing suits. Isaac put his arm around Michael as they walked from the kitchen.

"Twelve years old," he said to his son. "How are things going for you, Son?"

"I'm good."

"I understand our neighbors have asked you to tend to their yards."

"Uh-huh."

"Do you want to do it?"

Michael looked up at his father, trying to get a read on what his answer should be. He knew after many conversations through his short life that Father wanted him to be honest.

"Yes. I do. I want to make money."

Isaac grinned. "Good. It will be a great experience. It won't be long before you'll be courting young ladies. You'll need a job, believe me."

"Girls? Yuck."

Isaac laughed. Then his laughter faded, and sadness flooded in. He fought it off, but not before Michael saw it.

"What is it, Dad?"

Isaac shrugged. "You'll be a man soon."

"Is that bad?"

"No. Not bad. For a parent, time can be a bittersweet thing."

A sharp knock at the door ended the moment. Isaac answered the door, and man about his age stood on their front step. He was a friendly man with a serious look on his face.

"Patrick! What brings you here?"

"Isaac," Patrick said.

He nodded at Michael. "Michael, how are you?"

"Fine."

Patrick looked back to Isaac. "There's been an . . . incident. You and I are on the enforcement team this month."

"I see," Isaac said.

Michael read his face and saw their beach plans leaving with this new visitor.

"We have the suspect at the town common, as usual," Patrick said. "The other enforcers are gathering."

"Very well. I'll get my cloak and meet you there. Thanks for letting me know."

Isaac started to shut the door. Patrick did not move.

"Something else, Patrick?"

Patrick glanced at Michael.

"Michael, will you excuse us?" Isaac said.

Michael took a step to leave.

"Actually, this concerns Michael," Patrick said.

Isaac glared at Patrick, who looked at Isaac as if he should know.

"He's turned twelve, yes?"

Isaac nodded as if accepting something he wanted to ignore.

"He has, and your point is taken. You go ahead. We'll catch up. Both of us."

Patrick said farewell, and Isaac closed the door.

"Dad, what did all of that mean?"

"Put on your cloak and walking shoes," Isaac said. "I need to speak to your mother."

Grace and the girls had to find something else to do with their day. They understood Isaac was called away sometimes. Grace was quiet upon learning Michael would go with Isaac this time. She had a bitter-sweet look on her face.

Michael waved goodbye to his mother and sisters. He turned and looked up at his father as they walked into the bright mid-morning sunlight. Isaac turned his face into the beam and smiled.

"Ah, the peace of sunlight," he said. "There was a time I feared I would never know it again."

Michael likewise turned his face to the sun. The warmth soaked into his chin and cheeks and he felt powerful.

"You have your walking shoes on?" Isaac asked.

"Yep."

"Speaking of times gone by, in the old days we had vehicles to take us from one place to the other."

"Huh?"

"Cars," Isaac said, wondering how to describe something to someone who had no idea what it was. "Like a teeny-tiny house that moved around, taking you here and there."

"Wow."

"You'd think 'wow,' but it was just another tool of complacency, taking away the thought that should go into action. Now, we walk to our destination. Not only is it good for the body, it's good for the mind. Gives us time for contemplation. Gives us our mind back. Gets us thinking about our purpose, the reason we go where we go."

"So where are we going?"

Isaac didn't answer right away. Michael waited, knowing his father was only searching for the right words.

"We're going to do our duty," Isaac finally said. "There's been a crime."

"Someone hurt someone or destroyed someone's things?"

"That's the bare bones of it."

"And I'm going?" Michael asked, excited.

"Yes. As Patrick pointed out, you are twelve. You have grown tall. Added muscle. You have the voice of a man. Nature has changed you from child to an adult. In the old days we denied this, setting arbitrary age levels to determine when a boy became a man or a girl became a woman. Now, we listen to nature."

"I'm a man?"

"Yes. But to make it official, you must perform the duties of a man, which you will do for the first time today."

"What do I have to do? Is it a test? I'm strong and can run fast!"

"It's not a competition, Son. Although you will need your strength."

Michael waited while his father gathered his thoughts.

"In the old days, for many, many years leading up to the Dark Times, the responsibilities of society were spread out among different, shall we say, specialized groups. If someone disrupted the moral or social order, they stood before each of these groups—police, the courts, the prisons, and if necessary, the executioner."

"A what?"

"An executioner is someone who kills those who have committed horrible crimes."

Michael felt an uneasy flutter in his stomach. "Oh."

"Anyway, at each step of the way in this legal process, someone new took over, and things were passed along to the next specialist. The police officer didn't see what happened to the person he arrested. Court members didn't enforce the death penalties they handed out. The executioner didn't mop up the blood he spilled. You see?"

Michael nodded, not caring much for what those words implied.

"Now, Son, with a chance to start over, those of us who came through the Dark Times, man and woman alike, realized we must take direct responsibility for the care and maintenance of a peaceful society."

"How?"

"You'll find out. Experience will be your teacher today."

They were silent for several minutes. Patrick waited for them at an intersection. He fell in with them as they all exchanged quiet hellos.

"Is it a man or a woman?" Isaac asked.

Patrick groaned. "Does it matter, Isaac?"

"I'm curious."

"Always details with you."

"Helps me prepare my mind."

"Very well. The accused is a man."

"Is he accused of crime against person or property?"

"Person," Patrick said. "The victim is a child."

Isaac's shoulders slumped.

"What's happened?" Michael asked, now wishing he could have stayed at home.

"Crimes against property are one thing," Isaac said. "Crimes against people, especially children, are severe, as are the penalties."

"The city gates were locked right away. There are witnesses," Patrick said.

"Do we know his location?"

"He's home."

Isaac looked surprised. Patrick shrugged.

"It's possible he acted in the heat of passion and knows escape and denial is futile," Patrick said.

"Or he is innocent and therefore refuses to act like a guilty man," Isaac said.

He turned to Michael. "Remember, Son, innocence is our presumption. For one day it might be you or I who stands accused."

"Still, there is a risk of bringing even an innocent man to trial," Patrick said. "You never know how they will react."

"Who is the accused?" Isaac asked.

"Vincent Beardley."

Isaac thought about him and nodded to himself.

"Are the three of us enough to bring him in?" Patrick asked.

"I believe so. Let's go take him to the common."

They were silent for the rest of the walk. Michael's apprehension grew as Patrick and his father knocked at the front door of Vincent Beardley's house. The door opened and a crying woman answered.

"Please! It can't be true! Don't take him."

Unseen arms pulled her aside and a tall man, Vincent Beardley, appeared before them.

"Patrick, Isaac," he said. "Looks like you two drew lots for public service."

He saw Michael standing behind them.

"Is this ritual for underage voyeurs now?"

"Michael is twelve," Isaac said. "He is a man. You will speak to him and about him as you would any of us."

Vincent snorted as if that didn't amount to much in the way of respect.

"Time is short, Vincent," Isaac said. "Please fetch your cloak and speak to your family. You know you might not be coming back."

Vincent glared at them, but ducked back into his house. Patrick and Isaac stepped away and joined Michael on the sidewalk. In seconds, muffled screams and wails broke through the walls of Vincent's house.

"Don't worry, Son," Isaac said. "Our duties are sometimes unpleasant."

The screaming and pleading continued.

"There is a lesson here. Before disrupting order, ask yourself, is it worth this?" Patrick asked, jerking his head toward Vincent's house.

Vincent came out with the sounds of sniffles and sobs behind him.

"I hope you're enjoying the anguish of my fam—"

"Let's go, Vincent," Isaac said. "Someone will come for them in a few minutes. If things go your way, you will sup with them tonight."

More men and women joined them as they drew near to the town common. They kept Vincent in the center of the growing crowd. There were greetings and small talk, but most stayed with their own thoughts until they reached their destination.

The town common was a wide, circular clearing in the center of the city. It was ringed with stone columns, and arched gates allowed entrance at the twelve, three, six, and nine o'clock points.

The robed members of the community arranged themselves in a circle. Vincent walked to the center and stood straight and defiant. Everyone in the walled city knew what to do according to their assigned roles when there was an incident. Isaac lowered his voice to speak to his son.

"Stay with Patrick, Michael. Watch and learn."

A sobbing man and a woman stood near the twelve o'clock gate. Others tried in vain to comfort them.

"Let us begin," Isaac said to the crowd.

Two men entered via the three o'clock gate carrying a stretcher. The sobbing couple became more hysterical. The men placed the stretcher on the ground ten feet away from Vincent as Isaac went to the couple. He placed a hand on each of their cheek.

"Please, my friends," he said. "I know your grief is beyond measure, but you might influence the vote of the jury. You know we can't have that."

The couple stopped crying and dried their faces. Isaac waited until their breathing returned to normal. They nodded at him. He turned to the crowd.

"Very well," he said. "There has been a crime against humanity. A rare occurrence here, but the dark impulses of humanity still dwell within us. We must be ready to do our duty to the moral order.

"Vincent Beardley!"

Vincent stood straight. Michael watched fascinated as the man's earlier arrogance vanished. This was serious business. If Vincent denied it before, he was well aware of it now.

"You stand accused."

Isaac gestured toward the covered stretcher on the ground.

"Look at the stretcher, Vincent. When the blanket is removed, do not look away, do not blink. Look at what is there. Do you understand?"

"I do."

"That goes for all of us," he said to the group, his eyes meeting Michael's. "Do not look away."

Isaac nodded to the men who had carried in the stretcher. They removed the blanket, revealing the body of a young girl. Michael stared at the body in shock, unable to imagine what caused such mess, such injury. The crowd gasped, but otherwise remained calm. Michael glanced at the grieving couple. Their faces contorted in anguish, but they didn't make a sound.

He looked at the body again, then at Vincent. The accused watched the body as he had been instructed. He was horrified, but something flashed across Vincent's eyes, something dark and unholy, something Michael didn't like at all. He looked to Isaac, already studying his son's response. Isaac saw the look of uncertainty in his son's eyes and nodded his approval.

"Who dares accuse me of this atrocity?" Vincent asked through clenched teeth.

"Bring the witnesses," Isaac said.

A couple with two children—Michael assumed them to be a family—came through the crowd and stood in the center, away from Vincent. Isaac moved close to them. He smiled, reassuring them.

"Thank you for coming, my friends. I am obligated to remind you that false testimony is as grave a crime to our existence as the destruction of this poor girl. Do you understand?"

The family members nodded, answering yes out loud.

Their testimony was devastating. In the dark, early morning hours, they had rousted themselves to go to the flat roof of their house and watch a meteor shower. Its approach had been well-known to the community. Michael knew of it, but his desire to see it was not strong enough to get him out of bed in the middle of the night.

Vincent tried to hide it, but Michael read it in his face—he didn't know about the meteor shower.

The family had noticed a man darting through the shadows of the neighborhood. The stranger had looked around, checking to make sure the streets were empty and the surrounding windows dark. It never occurred to him to check the rooftops. The stranger ran between the family's house and the neighboring one. In the alley, he picked up something limp and floppy—a small body. The lurker then stepped into a wide beam of moonlight. He stared up into the light as if cursing it, then ran away and out of sight. The moon was so bright the father could see the pink toenail polish on the small feet of the body—the same as the dead girl lying before them.

"And the stranger's face?" Isaac asked. "Did the moonlight show you that?"

"Yes," the father said. "It was Vincent Beardley, who stands here now."

"A filthy lie!" Vincent yelled.

"Be quiet, Vincent," Isaac said. "Your turn will come."

Isaac turned to the family. "Now, you realize that falsely accusing a man puts you at risk of punishment for that crime?"

"We do."

Isaac strolled around the center, coming to face Vincent.

"We have heard eyewitness testimony from citizens of good standing. What say you, Vincent?"

Vincent, shaken, held his ground.

"I, too, am a citizen of good standing," Vincent said, addressing the crowd. "I've always come to my neighbors' aid. Never stolen. I've worked hard for everything I have. What am I to do? Claim I was sleeping when this happened? Summon my family to testify that they, too, slept through the night, as any normal person would do? You demand proof of sleep in exchange for my own life in front of people who believe me a child killer? Is this justice?"

"You deny it then?" Isaac asked.

"Of course I deny it. The midnight gaze of rooftop star watchers proves nothing. Darkness and distance? None of you can condemn a man on such shaky testimony."

Isaac turned to the family. "Is there anything else we should know?"

"Perhaps it was a werewolf enjoying the moon!" Vincent said.

"The man we saw was shirtless," the father of the witness family said. "On his back was a set of scars."

"All of us who lived through the Dark Times have scars, for crying out loud!"

Isaac summoned two people from the gathered—Patrick and Michael. Patrick went to the father, who whispered to Patrick the details of the scars. Michael went to Vincent. The accused gave Michael a sour look, but raised his cloak to let Michael see his back, out of view of Patrick.

Patrick and Michael met in the center of the small area and conferred.

"Did he have scars?" Patrick asked.

"Yes. Shaped like triangle with a dot in the middle," Michael said.

"And the bottom of the triangle is the longest line of the scar?"

"Yes."

Patrick walked behind Vincent and confirmed the witness's description. He nodded solemnly at Isaac. Seeing that, Vincent's shoulders sank, and his breathing quickened.

"Vincent, have you anything else to say?" Isaac asked.

"Only that if you proceed, you condemn an innocent man."

Isaac gave Vincent the last word and assembled a jury from the gathered. Six men and women. Michael and Patrick were among those he picked. Vincent also picked six. The twelve gathered at the six o'clock gate to debate Vincent's fate. Everyone waited in silence.

Michael stood in the group and listened as they deliberated Vincent's fate. A few of them protested his innocence to provide advocacy on his behalf. There was, however, little doubt of his guilt when the eyewitness evidence and scars were taken into account. The discussion was shorter than Michael expected.

"We must decide," said one man. "Let us take a vote. Remember, if he is guilty, we must say so with conviction, even though it means Vincent's death at our hands."

Michael felt sick. He knew Vincent was guilty, but to condemn him to death? And what did "at our hands" mean for Michael?

The first three jurors pronounced Vincent guilty. Michael felt the stares of his fellow jury members. He glanced at Vincent, who stared ahead into nothing. There was no avoiding his vote. Vincent was a child murderer, the victim not much younger than Michael's own sisters.

"Guilty," Michael said.

The vote was unanimous. Even the jurors picked by Vincent voted against him. They broke ranks and came to the center of the ring, gathered around the family, and escorted them out through the twelve o'clock gate. Had Vincent been ruled innocent, he would have been escorted out, and the family left to face trial for false accusation. Vincent's family became hysterical.

"Be silent if you want to say farewell!" Isaac said.

They got themselves under control just enough to say an awful goodbye before they were dragged from the ring. Michael's breathing sped up, and he had to look away. Patrick appeared at his side and put a soothing hand on his shoulder.

"It's our duty, Michael. Thankfully, we don't have to do this often."

Vincent's family was gone. The girl's body was taken away. Vincent stood alone and condemned. Michael stood with the jury near the gate where the accusing family had left.

Patrick placed a large canvas bag on the ground near the jury members. He took large pairs of gloves from the bag and they passed it around until every member had a pair. Michael received his and slid them on his hands. They were like boxing gloves, only smaller, with less padding and heavy. Strips of metal and wood were tied around the outside of the gloves.

Isaac watched the jury put on their weighted gloves. Michael's eyes met his, and his father's expression told him to be strong. When the jury was ready and still, Isaac faced Vincent, his face cold and stony.

"You are condemned as a murderer by your fellows. You have forfeited your humanity."

Isaac stepped away from Vincent and stood with the others along the rim of the ring.

Vincent shook as the jury walked to him. Michael looked at the other jury members, his father, Vincent. His stomach tightened with fear, but his heart raced and surged blood to his brain and muscles. He glanced at his father again, who nodded in satisfaction at the aggressive posture now taken by his son. The looks on the faces of the other jurors were likewise savage and grim. They surrounded Vincent.

Vincent shouted at them. "Well, get on with—"

A right hook from a juror cut him off. Vincent staggered back, holding his face, blood spurting.

"Murderer!" shouted another as he delivered a blow to Vincent's stomach.

They were on him at once, fists swinging, shouts and curses. Vincent kept his feet as long as he could, pinballing between hooks and jabs. Michael watched in shock, but hadn't yet thrown a punch. He looked at his father, who nodded at him to participate.

Michael stepped through the tight crowd and threw a punch that landed on Vincent's nose and sent him to the ground. Now the murderer absorbed kicks and punches. Michael joined in the assault, land-ing several solid kicks and blows. The wood and metal of the gloves tore skin and muscle and released streams of blood.

Vincent lost consciousness, but the attack continued until Isaac stepped in and called a halt. The jurors stood back and caught their breath as Isaac checked Vincent's pulse. Feeling nothing, he stood and faced the gathered.

"It's done."

Michael looked at the dead man, battered and lying on a spreading blanket of blood.

"You've done your duty," Isaac said. "Return to your normal mind."

The jurors took off their gloves, which Patrick collected. Michael studied their faces. No one was triumphant. There had been no cheers while the assault played out. Only the grim looks of people who had no choice but to do a dirty job.

A group of men and women brought a stretcher, a bucket of water, and several mops. A juror gestured to Michael for help, and he helped the man lift and place Vincent's body on the stretcher. Together, the jury mopped the blood until the center ring was as clean as before. Michael helped mop the blood and then went with the jurors to the cemetery with the body. There, Michael took a shovel and dug a grave with two other men and a woman. When the hole was deep enough, he and Patrick tossed Vincent's body into it.

By then exhausted, Michael shoveled dirt over the body until the ground was level again. The tools were taken away, and everyone left to return to their lives. Michael stood by the grave. Isaac joined him there. It was lunchtime.

"The first one is hard," Isaac said. "Life becomes complicated as we grow older."

"Will there be others?"

"You can count on it. Not many, but every generation has those who surrender to the urge to destroy."

"Didn't we destroy Vincent?"

"To maintain order and civilization, we must be prepared to be more savage than the worst monster among us. You found the savage within. Now you must keep it in a cage until it's needed again."

Michael nodded, staring at the grave.

"You have misgivings," Isaac said. "Everyone does the first time. Stay here until they pass. And when they do, leave your misgivings here. Forever. Then come home."

Isaac walked away, back toward their house.

Michael stared at the disturbed earth of the murderer's grave.

There's a Clown at the Door

"Dad, there's a clown at the door."

Steve sighed at the unusual sentence from his 9-year-old son, Dennis. He sat up on the couch he'd been laying on for the past two hours, engrossed in a ball game.

"What?" he asked, his voice straining to maintain a patient tone.

"There's a clown at the door." Dennis sounded serious.

Steve could not see the front door from his seat. The innocent seriousness in his son's face lightened Steve's mood.

"What does he want?"

Lila had been on him lately for chastising Dennis for telling such whoppers as "there's a clown at the door." It is just his imagination, she said, and when you get on him, you stifle his creativity. She suggested playing along while trying to steer him toward reality.

"He wants to take Molly for a ride."

Molly, Dennis' 2-year-old sister. Steve chuckled. *That kid.* He considered ordering his son to come sit beside him for a fatherly talk about the dangers of telling fibs, even in jest. However, the sounds of a roaring stadium crowd from the television refocused his energy, and he eased back into the couch. The boy wants to play with his sister. Nothing wrong with that.

"Okay, fine. Let him take Molly for a ride. Be careful."

Maybe Lila was right. Sometimes it's best to keep the peace and let kids be kids. No harm in a child inhabiting a world of his own creation. Steve had been there once himself and had long ago watched his imagination shrink away in favor of more practical thoughts. One can go too far in either direction. Just let him be a kid while he can. There'll be plenty of time to be boring.

Dennis' pajama-covered feet thumped up the stairs. By the time he returned, Steve was once again oblivious to everything but down and yardage.

No sound from Dennis through halftime, but not two minutes into the third quarter, his lazy Monday night was interrupted again.

"Dad, the clown's back."

Steve stretched. "What does he want now?"

"He wants to take Patrick for a ride, too."

"Patrick, eh?"

"Yep."

"First your little sister, and now your little brother?"

"Uh-huh."

"Where is the clown going to take them?"

"I don't know. Just for a ride."

"When is he bringing them back?"

"He isn't."

Steve sat up and looked at his son with bemused curiosity. "You mean he is going to keep them?"

"I guess."

"Well, why don't you go ask the clown what he plans to do with your brother and sister if he isn't bringing them back."

"Okay."

Before Steve could say another word, Dennis ran off toward the front door. He heard his son scamper through the patio. The front door creaked open and Dennis spoke. Steve listened with small concern for another voice, but heard no one else. He chuckled to himself as Dennis came trotting back into the living room.

"Well?"

"He said he isn't bringing them back because he's hungry."

Steve's face drew into a offended scowl. "Dennis, that's taking your game a little too far."

"Sorry," Dennis said with the voice of the unfairly accused.

Steve rubbed his temple, his wife's words ringing in his conscious.

"Can Patrick go too?" his son prodded.

"Okay, fine," Steve said. "Have fun with your game, but play nice and be careful."

Dennis ran off again.

Steve returned to his game and threw his arms up in frustration as the replay showed the trick play paying off big. He quaffed the last warm swallow of beer and considered going for another when he heard soft footsteps again. *That kid.* Steve grinned to himself, wondering where Dennis's imaginative mind might take him.

It was peaceful for another hour before Dennis approached once again.

"Dad—"

"What does the clown want now?"

"He wants mom to go with him."

"Well, you don't have to ask me for that. Go ask her."

Have a taste of your own medicine, Sweetheart. Haha.

"She's asleep," Dennis said.

"In that case, don't wake her up."

"But what should I tell the clown?"

Steve felt himself stepping to the edge of his patience. When would this kid tire of his relentless fantasizing?

"Tell the clown to go wake your mother up and ask her himself."

Steve chuckled as Dennis jogged off.

The crowd erupted in cheers again, and Steve woke with a start. He glanced at his watch—he'd dozed for twenty minutes. A loud thump sounded from upstairs. Steve sat up.

"Dennis?" he said.

Dennis ran into the living room. "Yeah?"

"What was that noise?"

"Oh, that's just the clown. He's up in your bedroom getting mom."

Steve sighed and rubbed his eyes. "Dennis, that's enough. It's time for bed. Now, I want you to stop the clown game. It's late, and I don't want you waking up your mother. You know she has to get up early every day."

"What should I tell the clown?"

Steve took a deep breath.

"Dennis," he said, making an effort at patience. "I want you to tell 'the clown' to bring everyone back and go home. It's time for you to go to bed."

"But, mom's just leaving for her ride with the clown!"

Steve didn't know how much longer he could play along. The escalating crowd noise told him he was missing another amazing play. He gave a dismissive wave of the hand. "Fine. Let mom take her ride, then it's bedtime. Understand?"

"Okay."

Steve sighed with relief as Dennis left. He had never seen such an active imagination, not even in himself when he was that age. He had just resettled himself into the couch when Dennis came into the living room again.

"Dad? Can I ask you one more thing?"

Steve summoned all his willpower. "Yes."

"The clown wants to know if you will go for a ride, too."

"No. I'm not getting up. Sorry. Tell him no."

Steve waited for a few seconds, wondering what kind of response his son was conjuring.

"He said he'll carry you. You don't have to get up."

Steve chuckled in helpless frustration. "Okay then. Tell the clown to get in here and carry me away."

Dennis ran out of the room. The front door opened.

People had tried to warn Steve and his wife about the energy drain of growing children. He had to smile in spite of himself at his young son's fantasy mind. Perhaps he would be famous for his creativity, make a comfortable living, and provide his dear old dad with a leisurely retirement.

The front door thudded shut. Dennis came back to the living room. Only this time, something was different. That wasn't the soft pat of his son's feet. These steps were much heavier, louder, and spaced further apart. He giggled to himself as he imagined his overly creative son trying his best to mimic the long, heavy strides of an adult. Steve shook his head as the footsteps reached the couch.

That kid.

Father's Bell

They sat together, mother and daughter, waiting in fearful silence. A candle flickered on the table between them as if it sensed the tension in the air. Mother tried to read by the dancing flame. Young Patrice sat in a wooden chair, too afraid to move. The slightest sound or movement from Father's bedroom made them flinch in terror.

The night was windy. Father didn't feed much anymore, but on the night he required it, the wind came first, followed by rain or snow, depending on the season. He used to leave when it was time to feed, but for many years now his body didn't work well enough for him to even leave his bed. In a long ago time, Mother and Patrice watched him leave and waited for his return. These days, they had to feed him, for his appetite had not diminished.

Mother re-read the same page for the fifth time. Concentration was impossible, but she did her best. Anything to get her mind off what they would soon have to do. She glanced out the window at the trees buckling in the cold, unmerciful wind. The gales had long ago stripped the trees of their leaves, leaving them of little use other than to cast ominous shadows through the windows.

"Do you think he will want a feeding tonight?"

Mother dropped her book at the sound of Patrice's voice stabbing through the silence.

"Good heavens!" Mother composed herself, speaking in whispers. "What kind of question is that? Of course he will."

"He didn't use it all last time," Patrice said. "Just made me wonder if he isn't as hungry these days."

"Well that's no reason to hold back. You know what he'll do."

Patrice tried to forget about what happened last time they held back.

A small bell hanging on the upper post of the bedroom door softly chimed. Normally an innocent, joyful sound. Here the summons of evil. Mother and Patrice looked at the bell, then each other.

"We best not wait," Mother said.

She stood and gathered her hat and coat.

Patrice sighed. "What will be my job tonight?"

"I worked the tools last night. Tonight that will be your job."

Patrice hated working the tools. However, venturing out for Father's meal was risky and exhausting.

Mother wrapped up and stepped out into the gusting darkness.

Patrice entered the kitchen and tugged at a heavy trunk under the large oak dining table. Inside the trunk was a medium-sized bundle wrapped in blue velvet, which she placed on the table. She unrolled the bundle and spread it on the table. There were saws of different lengths with teeth of varying size. Plenty of knives, which she sharpened to perfection. She noticed a spot of something dark and wet on one of the saws. Mother had not done a proper clean up. Father would be displeased. She soaked a washcloth and cleaned the saw.

After the tools were ready, Patrice checked the restraints at either end of the table. People disliked the tools in a way Patrice understood but could not sympathize.

Satisfied the equipment was ready, Patrice took her seat again. She wiped sweat from her forehead and caught her breath. The tool work was tedious, but at least it was indoors and much safer.

Footsteps on the front walkway sounded through the wind. Patrice opened the front door for her Mother. Mother came in breathing fast and carrying a large sack. She was satisfied, but a little worried.

"Smaller than usual," Patrice said, noticing the size of the object in the sack.

"Large enough," Mother said. "We are running out of food, and we must do our best."

"If only Father could be reasoned with."

"Keep your voice down, Child," Mother said in a panic.

"One of the saws was unclean."

Mother's face went pale.

"Did you tell Father?"

"No. I cleaned it."

Mother sighed in relief. "Very well. For that I will help you work the tools tonight."

They put it on the table and fastened the restraints. This one struggled hard. In spite of its mouth being covered, it made a lot of noise. Its struggles caused a mess to rival any other. Patrice never saw one who so hated the tools. They would clean for most of the night.

"Why didn't we use the club on it?" Patrice asked.

"You keep repeating that silly question and the answer never changes: Father likes it fresh."

Patrice began the cleaning while Mother took Father his meal. When Mother returned, they cleaned together until the candles had burned low. They rested when they were done. Over the years they had learned to sleep sitting upright in their chairs. Their beds hadn't been used in a long time. They didn't dare venture too far from Father's bell. One never knew when he would ring for a feeding. Mother bore horrible scars beneath her dress to show what happened when Father's bell went unanswered.

Two days and nights passed, and their anxiety grew. It was long past time for Father to have rung for his scraps and used dishes to be taken away. Mother stared at the door, then the bell. The air outside was still. There was no sound.

"Patrice, you haven't heard the bell since last night, have you?"

"No, Mother. Am I a fool who would ignore the bell?"

"Something must be wrong."

Mother paced, unsure what to do. She walked to the door and placed her hand on the knob, then quickly took it away. She also bore scars from entering when she wasn't summoned. But what would be the price for ignoring Father if he needed her?

"I'll go," Patrice said.

Mother nodded, weary, knowing it was wrong to let Patrice go into the room unbidden, but lacking the courage to go herself. She stood aside and let Patrice enter the room.

Mother did not even pretend to be interested in reading. She sat in her chair, waiting and listening. No sounds came from the room. Mother couldn't decide if that was good or bad, if she had seen Patrice for the last time or not. After an eternity measured in minutes, Patrice exited the room, looking unharmed and unconcerned.

"Well?" Mother was about beside herself with anxiety. "Did you receive instruction?"

Patrice nodded.

It was easier to subdue Mother than Patrice expected. She was young and growing strong as she approached her peak of youth and vitality. Mother was on her downhill march and no match for her daughter's power. Not without struggle, Mother was on the table, fastened to the restraints. She struggled in vain against the bonds. Patrice giggled to herself. Mother should know the restraints never let anyone go. She made an awful noise when Patrice rolled out the tool bundle. The sounds of Mother's voice and the terror in her eyes stirred a remnant of pity on Patrice's heart. She almost got the club to make it fast and merciful, but decided against it.

Father was hungry. Father liked it fresh.

Welcome to the Lake

Drunken Irishmen!

Casey Mullen cursed his kinsmen for the bizarre street layout of the Lake Christopher community. He looked left and right to try to make sense of his surroundings. The streets curled around the many houses and into other curves and splits and roundabouts and out of sight.

To be honest, the designers did the best they could with the odd shape of the lake. It looked like two ink blots from the air. A large blot to the north and a smaller one to the south. The two bodies of water joined in the middle by a small strait. A bridge covered the strait and linked the two sides of the lake.

The houses of the lake settlement lined the water's edge and sprawled out into the surrounding Iowa countryside. The roads followed the houses as they sprouted up through the years according to the whim of their builders. Street signs stood along the obvious north-south/east--west pathways, but of course the strange loop-de-loops and whoop-de-doos were unmarked. That's why Casey grumbled about his brethren.

His car had shredded its serpentine belt on a desolate highway, which left most of his engine components crippled. He had struggled to get the vehicle to the shoulder and waited an hour for someone to drive by before deciding to hoof it and hope he found civilization. Having traveled from Illinois for a wedding, he didn't know the area. The remote location had no available data networks.

Empty fields and forbidding forests passed by, but no cars or people, or even animals. His alarm grew. The only disturbance to the silent isolation was a sonic boom that startled him. He checked the skies for a military jet, but didn't see one. Probably too high in the air.

A one-hour walk brought him to the lake. He knocked on the doors of the outer circle of houses, but no one answered. He walked further in, knocking on some doors and passing by others. The houses he walked past had a downright spooky look to them, as if built and designed to keep strangers away. The front doors hid around corners and behind fences and high porches. He was happy to keep his distance, if that was the plan.

All the houses, normal and not-so-normal, looked expensive. Lakefront property and seclusion cost money. Their yards weren't simple squares of green grass. They were science fiction landscapes of mulch, rock, statuary, shrubs, and rare flowers.

He spotted a house with a carved wooden sign hung under the porch light: *Welcome to the Lake.* Most houses had a variant of this sign. A few did not. The friendly message of the sign did not translate to an answered door, so he moved on.

Thinking there might be an event happening at the lake that might explain everyone's absence, he stopped and listened for sounds of revelry he might trace to the source. The air was still, and there was not a peep of a human voice. Come to think of it, Casey realized there were no joggers, no children playing, no lawn mowers roaring. Complete silence. No one to give him directions. No central office or community center that might have a knowledgeable person at a desk. A wave of unease swept over him, and he decided it would be best to suck it up and take the long walk back to his car and wait for help.

He looked at the winding roads again and realized he had no idea how to return to the lake's entrance. He felt like a man who woke up on another planet, or a hapless fellow from The Twilight Zone who missed that signpost up ahead and entered forbidden territory. It was the last day of April and a chill still filled the air. He faced a shivery night if he had to sleep under a tree.

"*Hey!*"

Casey flinched at the sudden whisper. He looked around, seeing nobody.

"*Over here!*"

The voice came from an ancient A-frame house with a sandy yard and tufts of cotton covering its deck. It had no welcome sign. A tall old man with white hair and an anguished expression opened the door and walked down his front step and to Casey.

"What the hell are you doing here, Son?" he asked. "Everyone knows not to come here. Especially not today, for the love of Pete!"

"Everyone?" Casey said, his frustration ready to burst. "Including people who have never been here?"

"An out-of-towner. Should have known."

"Sir, my car broke down and I'm looking for a tow. If you don't have a phone or don't want to share it, I'd love nothing more than to leave, if you'll kindly point the way."

"Out on the highway, I take it?"

"Pretty sure."

The old man nodded. "Fine. I'll call for a truck, but you can't wait here."

"Good enough, and thank you."

"I'm going to flail my arms and raise my voice, but don't take it personal. It's just for show. People are watching, so play along."

Casey took a step back as the old man gave him directions out of the lake while looking as though he was yelling in fury. Casey cowered on cue.

"Take this road 'til it dead ends. That's the outer road. Take that to the second left, which will lead you to the bridge. Go over the bridge and stay on the straight road, and by straight I mean it will do a couple of s-curves but don't wander off the center path. At the next dead end take a left and you're on the road out."

"Okay, thanks," Casey said, thinking there was no way he would remember all of that.

"It's getting late. It's getting dark. If you're a jogger, run. If not, I'd advise you to take it up."

The old man turned away and returned to his house. Casey stared after him, worrying he'd look like an idiot running in loafers and khakis, but there was a clear sense of danger now, so jog he did.

It only took moments to get lost again. Casey had no skill at remembering complicated directions, but he figured he was good for the first few turns. He still hadn't found the bridge yet. Darkness fell fast. He waited for street lights to come on, and it was only then he noticed there were no light posts. The houses remained dark. No glowing bedroom lights or porch lights. Only the full moon on a cloudless night lit the quiet settlement, casting long shadows that cut through the cold, silver beams.

He finally found the bridge. The old man had told him to go straight from there, but at the other end he found the road split off in two directions. Had the old man lied to him? Unlikely. He obviously wanted Casey to get out of there. Did he not know the layout of his own neighborhood? Also unlikely. Had an unknown magic of the lake rearranged the road?

Casey shrugged to himself as he thought of that. It had been such a surreal day that nothing would surprise him. Either way, he had to choose which way to go, and both roads looked as though they led deeper into the trees and houses. He thought he might cry.

He turned to lean against the bridge railing and ponder his next move. The water splooshed beneath him as a fish flopped about. He grinned in spite of his anxiety. Then a second splash, this one louder and leaving a huge rippling wake. Casey stood straight and backed away from the railing. The deep ripple sped into what looked to be the large side of the lake, reflecting moonlight onto the surrounding houses. He speculated on what it could be. His guess was a large catfish.

A loud bell clanged in the distance. Casey leapt back from the railing. Now what?

"He comes every year about this time."

Casey nearly jumped out of his shoes at the soft voice, his nerves thoroughly shot. A kindly-looking old woman approached him on the bridge. She wore a black robe. The hood was down. She used a cane.

"Not sure why," she said. "Maybe he likes the weather. Maybe he likes where we are against the sun. We all have our ideas."

She chuckled at his appearance.

"I'm sorry, Dear. I've startled you."

He smiled, gathering himself. "Yes. I was starting to think no one lived here."

"You caught us on a busy day, I'm afraid. Are you lost?"

"Very. Just trying to get back to my car. Can you point the way?"

"Oh, I'd be happy to. If it's okay with him."

She nodded toward the lake, at the rippling wake that continued into the distance.

"I'm sorry," Casey said. "All this talk about 'he' and 'him'. . . you mean something in the water?"

"He first came in the sixties," she said. "Took many of our children. Awful, awful year. Happened again the year next. Some of us got together and, you might say, reached out with our minds. We heard him speak. A deal was made. We give him one per year, and that's good enough for him."

"Ma'am—"

"Oh, you can call me Norma."

"Norma. Who or what is he?"

She let out a grandmotherly laugh. "We don't know! He's not from around here."

"I see."

He looked around, feeling afraid as ever. Several men and women in hooded robes now stood at both sides of the bridge. He was trapped. An awful vision of being tossed over the bridge and into the fanged maw of an alien water beast was a real possibility. Only this afternoon he had been in his car, listening to an audiobook.

At a loss for words, he tried to think about how he would fight his way out.

"Let's go, Hon. There's no getting away."

Several men of the group closed ranks around him.

"You being here today of all days isn't an accident. Don't worry. If he doesn't want you, you can go."

They didn't toss him over the bridge. Instead, they gestured for him to follow Norma. She set an agonizingly slow pace, but the others patiently walked behind her. He noticed with much confusion that the split road leading from the bridge was now a single path again.

A boathouse faded into view, its entrance hidden in the shadows. Norma entered. Casey looked around, knowing escape was unlikely once he went in. Strong hands shoved him forward. He had no choice.

Matches crackled to life as the group lit candles. The soft, flickering light revealed the interior of the stone boathouse. Along with gas cans, paddles, rope and other boathouse items, strange symbols and unknown writing covered the walls. The floor ended where the water began. A square of chain link fence spanned the open area. The water lapped and splashed through the criss-crossing metal. Chain restraints led to the four corners.

"Bring her out," Norma said.

Casey heard swhimpering as the group dragged an adolescent girl out of the crowd. She fought her handlers, who held her tight and brought her to the fence to chain her down. Her eyes met Casey's and, seeing he was also a captive outsider, she pleaded with him for help.

He took a visual inventory of everything in the boathouse, searching for something, anything, that might help them both. It wasn't easy to see in the flickering candlelight, but there were plenty of potential weapons.

"Chain her," Norma said. "If he's still hungry after her . . ."

Her eyes met Casey's, kind yet malevolent.

". . . He can have more. He can be unpredictable."

The girl screamed as the men dragged her close to the water. Waves churned and frothed as something agitated beneath. The panicked girl looked at Casey again, screaming for help as the robed people chuckled.

"No one can hear you clear out here, Honey," Norma said. "We are far away from anyone else. Now stop fussing. It happens pretty fast. Won't hurt much."

One man hugged the girl tight from behind while the other took a manacle and gestured to bring the girl to him.

Casey, noticing his two handlers absorbed in the girl's ordeal, yanked his arms free from their hands, raised his fists in the air, and drove them into each man's scrotum. They doubled over in pain, and the momentary shock of the others gave Casey enough time to grab a gas can and run out of the boathouse. He snatched Norma's lit candle as he passed.

The group chased him, but stopped short at the entrance to the boathouse when he brandished the candle and the gas can. The threat was clear.

"Send out the girl," he said.

"We can't do that, Honey," Norma said. "And you're not going to set us all on fire. You'll kill her, too!"

"I think you'll send her out," Casey said. "I've had a look at what you'll do for self-preservation. Send her out."

"No, Dear."

"Okay, then."

Casey tipped the gas can and poured it out in a slow trickle. The group gasped as the flammable liquid flowed toward their feet.

"If you don't like the fire, just jump in the water and swim away," Casey said. "I'm sure that thing isn't fast enough to eat all of you before you get to the shore."

Norma sighed. "Let her go."

The others looked at her and grumbled. The thrashing in the water behind them grew more ferocious with each passing second.

"They'll never find their way out. Let her go, and we'll bring them back later."

With arrogant assurance, they parted and the girl came out.

"Walk around the gas, Sweetie," Casey said.

She tiptoed around the wet pavement on her bare feet.

"Come on, let's go," he said. "Stay close."

He carried the candle and gas can with him.

"We'll see you in a few minutes, Hon," Norma called after them.

Casey poured a trail of gas behind them to give them a running start.

They rounded a curve and the boathouse was out of sight. In seconds they heard the angry growls and footfalls of the mob in pursuit.

"Where's that damn bridge?" Casey asked out loud.

"This way!" the girl said.

She led him through a series of lefts, rights, and curves until the bridge opened before them. Casey laughed when he saw it.

"How did you know?" he asked.

"They led me through here like a parade," she said.

"What's your name?" he asked.

"Brittany."

"We're gonna get you home, Brittany, but there's something we need to do first."

Casey emptied the gas can on the wooden planks, pouring as they walked backward across the bridge. He shook out the remaining drops and tossed the can onto the lake.

The group ran around a corner and toward them just as he touched the candle's flame to the spilled petrol. Orange and yellow flames burst from the soaked wood and in seconds the entire bridge was a bonfire.

Casey looked behind them. The path wound away toward a distant dead end, just as the old man told him it would. That was their way out.

Two men carried Norma to the front of the group and set her down. For the first time, she looked distressed.

"Come on," Casey said to Brittany, taking her hand.

"You'll never find your way out!" Norma yelled.

"I think we will," Casey said. "You're cut off from this side of the lake now. If you want to chase us, you'll have to swim for it."

Everyone looked into the lake water. The unknown creature swam toward them, his location given away by the deep, churning wake. Casey read the terror in every face.

Casey and Brittany turned to leave, walking instead of running.

"You're condemning us to death," Norma said.

They pleaded and begged.

"Imagine that," he said.

"We had an accord with him. If we break it, he'll kill us all. Every single one of us."

"It's your bed," Casey said. "Sleep in it."

They fled into the night, running nonstop until they were back to the highway. The lakeside community glowed orange under the spreading flames. Wails and screams carried across the flat plains. It was deep in the night by the time they reached his car.

A few days later, after an adventure of getting to safety and getting his car repaired, Casey drove the girl home to Colorado. He let her off in her driveway and watched from a distance as her family welcomed her in. He slept well that night, despite his dreams of pealing bells and splashing water.

Threads

Things change in the blink of an eye. What had begun as a fun night out for the six of them had descended into fearful silence inside the SUV. The rain had been steady and the clouds dark. A check of the radar via their smartphones had shown the storm heading northeast, so they decided to drive back to their meeting place on the other side of the big city. But the storm shifted southeast as if it had noticed them. They navigated through town as the wind and hail bore down upon them. Torrents of rain brought visibility to less than ten feet. Lightning flashed and spider-webbed through the clouds, adding macabre pyrotechnics to the scene. Warning sirens screamed a continuous blast, indicating a tornado sighted by radar or human eye. An ear-splitting electronic alarm came from the radio, followed by the barely-coherent voice on the radio telling everyone that the National Weather Service has issued . . .

"Monte, we've got to pull over," Sandy said.

Monte, his hands white-knuckled on the wheel, shot an irritated look at his wife.

"Where do you suggest we go?" he asked.

In the back of the SUV were Alan and Rebecca. The two couples were married and longtime friends. The two in the middle, Paul and Ginny, were out on their first date on the arrangement of the other two couples. They had never met, and the night had taken a turn for the tense.

"We're in the business district," Rebecca said. "The stores have probably shut their doors."

"But the siren!" Sandy said. "There's a tornado!"

"It could be anywhere in the county!" Monte said.

Sandy screamed and pointed out beyond the driver's window. Gasps and curses followed as everyone saw the immense tornado tear into a superstore just off the road to their left.

"Turn around!" Alan yelled.

Debris swirled into the air as the twister tore the massive structure apart.

Wood planks and bricks bounced off the road ahead of them and pelted their vehicle.

"Too late!" Monte said.

"There!" Rebecca said, pointing to a turnoff on their right. "That convenience store. Its lights are on. It's still open!"

"Go!" Sandy said.

Paul and Ginny, strangers to each other and unsure of their place in this dynamic, held hands and kept quiet.

Monte sped toward the corner store. The others watched in terrified awe as the tornado, not yet sated even after leveling a vast brick and concrete building, continued toward them.

The Escalade slid to a stop on the wet pavement, the doors opening before she came to a full stop. Alan looked back. The tornado churned across the street. Swirling, horizontal waves of brown and black clouds filled their vision. The six of them struggled to reach the front entrance as the vortex pulled at them. Corrugated metal sheets, trash bins, shopping carts, fast food bags, and even a clothing rack sailed past.

They ducked and dodged and pulled each other's collars, arms, and belts to help each other through the door. It took only seconds for them to get inside, although it felt like hours. The walls shook, but cut off the wind. They ran to the back and found the basement door. The last of them danced down the stairs as they heard an explosion followed by the chimes of falling shards of glass. They continued into the basement as the tornado flattened the building above them. Everyone huddled in a corner near surplus paper goods as a sound like a freight train plowing through a mountain of trash cans split their ears. The floor—their ceiling—held firm. The power gave out and they sat in blackness. After five unbearable minutes, the tornado moved on. The noise died away, replaced by the steady pattering of the rain.

As one their bodies relaxed and their hands and arms released the iron grips they'd held on each other. Paul and Ginny shifted apart. Their quickened breathing returned to normal and a sense of calm entered the darkness.

"Everyone okay?" Alan asked.

Everyone mumbled assurances.

Rebecca laughed. "That was close."

"One of us should have stood out there and recorded it," Monte said. "Like those idiots on YouTube."

A white glow pierced the blackness. Sandy's face appeared in a spectral glow above her phone. The others turned on their gadgets, too. The basement lit up with the equivalent light of a small lantern. They tried to dial emergency services.

Sandy shook her head. "Nothing. Anyone having any luck?"

No one had any luck.

"The networks are overloaded," Alan said. "We're on our own for the moment."

"The tornado went over," Ginny said. "Think it's safe to go out?"

"The twister could still drop debris behind it," Alan said.

"Wouldn't hurt to take a peek," Sandy said.

Alan aimed his phone light at Monte. "What do you say? Want to take a peek?"

Monte nodded and the two of them ascended the stairs. The others heard them rattle the door and knew what the score was before they got the report.

"Blocked," Monte said as they came back.

"Do you need help?" Rebecca asked.

"I think the Escalade is blocking it, Honey," Alan said.

"Going to take more people then," she said.

They flinched when a chunk of debris fell onto the floor above.

"Lord, my nerves are shot," Sandy said.

"I guess we have to wait," Ginny said. "I have music downloaded on my phone."

"That would be wonderful," Rebecca said.

"I wouldn't worry," Monte said. "The phone networks will clear up soon enough. We can call for help then."

"Some of us will make it," Paul said.

It was the first he'd spoken since they took shelter. Everyone looked in the direction of his voice. He had not activated his phone, and he sat in darkness.

"Well, that's a cheery thing to say," Alan said.

"Good Lord, Paul. Way to keep us calm," Sandy said.

"Everyone lives under a death sentence," Paul said. "All of us. I can see it now."

Alan aimed his phone beam at Paul. The others did the same. Ginny screamed.

Paul had a 12-inch section of a metal bar through his head. It protruded from either temple in equal lengths. The left side was clean; the right was bloody, thus showing the direction the bar traveled through his skull.

Everyone gathered around, bathing his head in the glow of their phones.

"Paul, are you okay?" Sandy asked.

"Yeah, fine. Smells like red in here."

"Oh my God," Sandy said.

"What's in his head?" Rebecca asked.

"Looks like a piece of a u-channel post," Alan said. "They use it for stop signs."

"Tornado must have done it," Ginny said.

"Is that possible?" Sandy asked.

"Tornadoes do weird things," Monte said. "They can put a straw through a tree."

"We have to get him help!" Sandy said.

She tried to dial emergency services again. "No dice."

"How is he still functioning?" Rebecca asked.

"Paul?" Monte asked. "Do you know you're hurt?"

Paul reached up and touched the exposed bar on either side of his head. He winced, and the others recoiled.

"Does it hurt?" Ginny asked.

"A little."

"I don't think the brain feels any pain," Alan said. "He's lucky for that much."

"I know our options are limited, but . . .what should we do?" Rebecca asked.

Everyone looked at everyone else. Alan cleared his throat.

"Not much we can do," he said. "He might be in shock."

"Should we try to take that thing out?" Monte asked.

"No way," Rebecca said. "It's in there tight. He needs surgery."

"And it's stopping any bleeding," Alan said.

He turned to Paul. "Are you comfortable, man?"

"I have a headache."

"I suppose so. Just keep sitting there. Can you do that?"

"Oh yes. I have decisions to make."

"About what?"

"Who will be at my side."

"We'll all be at your side," Ginny said.

Paul grinned as if she were a child saying silly things.

"They'll move the Escalade out of the way in about two hours," he said.

"How the hell do you know that?" Alan asked.

"It's in the sphere. I can see lots of stuff happening. Makes me dizzy. Sorry, I have to close my eyes to make sense of it."

Paul closed his eyes and laid back against a package of paper towels. He appeared to sleep.

"Wow, he took a shot," Monte said.

"Should we let him sleep?" Rebecca asked. "What if he doesn't wake up?"

"Let me see if I can look up what to do," Sandy said, thumbing commands into her phone. "Dammit. Still no signal."

"If he wants to sleep, I say let him sleep," Alan said.

"Agreed. It's best he's kept still," Monte said.

Ginny looked around. "We're in the basement of a convenience store. Not to be insensitive to Paul's situation, but I could use a beer. Even if it's warm."

"That's a good idea," Sandy said. "We can leave money for whatever we use."

"Works for me," Monte said. "I'm hungry. Let's find the snack cakes."

"I'll stay with Paul," Alan said.

He turned to his wife, Rebecca. "Babe? You'll get me some chips?"

"Sure. You want a beer?"

"Heineken."

The four of them fanned out through the bowels of the store to see what they could find. The beams of light danced ahead of them as they disappeared around a corner. Alan turned to check on Paul, and jumped when he saw Paul's eyes open, staring at him.

"Dammit! You scared me."

"Sorry."

"How are you feeling?"

"Not bad. Getting a sense of calm. Of finality."

"Finality? Hey, calm down, my friend. You'll be fine. Only a matter of time before the networks are back up and we can call for help."

"They'll be up in ninety minutes."

"How do you know?"

"It's already happened."

"Right. Listen, we don't have to talk now. You should rest."

"I'm sorry things didn't turn out differently for you and Rebecca."

"Paul, I know you have a head injury, but you should think before you speak."

"Just the messenger."

"Think. Then speak."

Paul was silent.

"Let's change the subject," Alan said. "What do you think of Ginny?"

"Very pretty. Very kind and nurturing."

"I told you you'd like her."

"She's infertile, though. That won't do."

"And you know this . . . how?"

"She told me."

"She told you she was infertile at dinner the first time you met?"

Paul chuckled. "No, Alan. She told me in three months. In this time thread, that is."

"This thread, huh?" Alan said. "How many are there?"

Paul's eyes went wide. "Oh, lots. Lots."

"Am I a millionaire in any of them."

"You sure are."

"Will I ever be in this one?"

"No."

"You don't play nice, do you?"

"Oh, I see. You think I'm raving because of a head injury?"

"Hey, man. We've been friends for a long time. So I won't bullshit you. Yes, you have a bad head injury and it's making you say strange things."

"I understand it sounds strange. But something has happened to me. Something beyond being hurt. It's awakened something. I can see the sphere, you know?"

"The sphere. Sure."

"I'm not here, I'm everywhere. I'm at all places and times. It's pretty cool, although it's overwhelming."

"You're not joking."

"Not at all."

Alan sat down and stretched out next to Paul.

"I suppose it doesn't hurt to let you think that," Alan said. "You'll be well soon enough."

"I am well. You see, all things flow through me now. Not many people reach this state. Just a freak thing, but here we are."

"I won't indulge this, Paul. You say what you think you need to say. I'm waiting for my beer and chips."

"Do you mind if I have Rebecca?"

"Rest up, Paul."

"She's fertile for her age. Why haven't you had children?"

"None of your business."

"Let me look through the threads," Paul said, concentrating with his eyes closed. "Ah, that makes sense."

"What do you mean?"

"You're sterile. Not in all threads, but this one. Sorry."

"The hell?"

"You should see the children she had with me."

Alan stood. "I can tell you won't shut up, and you're not at death's door, so I'm going to leave you."

"I need Rebecca, Alan. Ginny is barren. Sandy is not compatible."

Alan sighed. "You know there are other women in the world, right?"

"Only these three women have converged with me here. A lot of paths have come together through this tornado, but only one can go forward. The rest of you will try to stop me. I can't let you."

Alan frowned. "That sounds ominous, Paul."

"Nothing personal."

Alan squatted in front of Paul. "Now listen. I know you're injured, but you're crossing the line. Rebecca is my wife. Put any other thoughts out of your bisected brain. Understand?"

"Do you believe in fate?"

Alan sighed. "No."

"Normally, there isn't one. Not until I converged into the sphere."

"I'm finding the others."

"I can tie any thread together. I can create fate."

"Fine. What fate do you create for me?"

"You really want to know?"

"If you promise to shut up."

"You were shot during a robbery five years from now. Rebecca becomes a widow. Well, in that time thread, anyway."

"You're speaking in past and present tense at the same time. You're talking garbage."

"But that's the time thread I need."

"The one where I get killed?"

"Yes."

"So you can have Rebecca?"

"Yes."

"I'll do you the favor of waiting until you recover, and then I'll kick your ass."

"Fair enough."

"And I don't plan on getting shot."

"Who does?"

"You want something to drink?"

Alan's body shook as three small holes tore open in his chest in rapid succession. Blood splattered the stacks of toilet tissue behind him. He looked at Paul in shock.

"Shot resisting a robbery. Like I said," Paul said.

Alan dropped to his knees, unable to speak. He looked down the hall where the others had gone.

"So Rebecca is free now. Free to be with me."

Alan looked around, wide-eyed. He collapsed to his side.

"I had to move that timeline and thread it in with this one. Very sorry."

Alan rolled onto his back, his breathing wet and erratic.

"I'll take care of Rebecca. Don't worry. The world will know her name, Alan. You couldn't have given her that."

Alan was still. Paul closed his eyes to sleep again and was unsure how long he had dozed before he heard the others coming back.

"We have alcohol, sugar and salt!" Sandy said. "You guys still here?"

Still in the dark, they swept their phone light across the storage area.

"Are you sleeping?" Monte asked.

They saw the pool of blood under Alan.

"Alan? Are you all right?" Rebecca asked, alarmed.

Everyone trained their lights on Alan. His chest wounds and red-soaked shirt were visible.

Rebecca screamed and ran to her husband.

"Sorry, Rebecca," Paul said, barely audible.

What did you do? What did you do?

She tried to help him, attempting CPR, applying pressure to the wounds. After a stunned few seconds, the others rushed to her side to see if there was anything to be done. Alan was still and unresponsive.

"He's dead," Paul said.

Rebecca lunged at Paul. Sandy and Monte held her back. She screamed curses and questions.

"Shot by robbers," Paul said.

The others frowned and looked at each other in confusion and Rebecca raged.

"You have a gun?" Monte asked.

"Of course not."

"Let me go!" Rebecca shook free and ran to the stairs.

She tripped on her way up, and beat on the blocked door, screaming for help. Sandy ran after her, trying to calm her. Ginny stood frozen. Monte squatted to check Alan's pulse. Verifying the obvious, he looked up at Paul. He checked Paul for a weapon. Paul didn't resist. Monte found nothing.

"Well?" Monte asked.

"Shot by robbers," Paul said. "I told you."

"Don't be cute."

Paul rolled his eyes. "I'm going to have to explain this to everyone, am I?"

"Afraid so."

Rebecca continued to weep and scream for help and rattle the blocked door as Sandy tried to talk her down.

"You're a nice girl," Paul said to Ginny. "And there are futures where we had a long, happy life together. But it won't work out here and now. You're barren, and I need children."

Ginny gasped and took a step back. "How do you know that?"

"You told me three years from now. A little long to wait on telling me something like that, but understandable."

"What?"

"Your injury has done something to you," Monte said.

Paul pointed at him, impressed. "Yes! You are the smart, intuitive one."

"Hallucinations, maybe," Monte said to Ginny.

"But I am infertile," Ginny said.

"Lucky guess," Monte said.

"You're smart and intuitive, but not fast," Paul said. "You'll catch on when it's too late, which is why you can't leave here, either."

Monte crossed his arms. "I doubt you'll damage me in your condition."

"What about Alan?" Ginny asked.

Rebecca's screams subsided to sobs as Sandy consoled her. They remained at the top of the stairs.

"Yes, what about Alan?" Paul asked. "I have no gun, so how did he get shot?"

"You found a gun and stashed it somewhere," Monte said. "But you're not moving from that spot. That I can guarantee you."

"There are many deaths. Many threads of time. I'm pulling them together into one unbreakable rope."

"Did you kill Alan?" Monte asked.

"He was already dead. As are you."

Monte clenched his fists.

"Be careful, Monte," Ginny said. "That blow to his head did something. He has powers. Somehow. I don't know."

Paul looked at Ginny, then slowly to Monte, grinning. "She's right."

"I'm dead, huh?" Monte asked.

"We all are."

"Some of us are more dead than others," Monte said, pointing to Alan's body.

"I see your point. Yes."

"How do I die?"

"You died in all sorts of ways. We all will."

"Why was Alan shot?"

"I had to pick a sudden death. Didn't have time to wait around for him to die of Alzheimer's as he does in several threads. That took years!"

"Why does it have to be sudden?" Ginny asked.

Paul watched her, seeing her body shaking, tears welling up.

"Because you're all going to stop me. In fact, you do stop me in other threads."

"How am I going to die?" she asked.

As if to answer, Ginny rose into the air as if the section of floor on which she stood lost gravity. She gasped, flailing her arms and legs. She rotated until her body was horizontal to the ground. Monte rushed to help her.

"I wouldn't do that, Monte."

Monte froze. Paul looked to Ginny.

"You die in a plane crash. It's the quickest option."

"No! Don't!" she pleaded.

"Killed on impact," Paul said. "So there's that."

Her scream cut off as she fell to the floor. Monte stared in shock at her torn body. She looked as if she'd been mangled in a plane crash. His breathing quickened, and he glared.

"So we're all doomed?" Monte asked.

"All but Rebecca."

"Why does she live?"

"She'll bear my children."

"Should we hear from her on that?"

"She'd probably say no, but she doesn't know she's already borne them. Several. I've seen them. I've seen much more."

"You're going to kill me then? Kill my wife, Sandy?"

"No. You're not listening. You're already dead. I'm just shifting things around."

"I'm sure it will all get sorted on Judgment Day. We'll see how you fare."

"I suppose."

Monte dove at Paul, reaching for the bar, grabbing it, trying to twist it, trying to break Paul's neck. Paul, much smaller in stature, offered feeble resistance.

"How am I going to die? Huh?" Monte raged.

Sandy and Rebecca ran back from the stairs.

"Sandy," Paul said, grimacing from the pain of Monte's attack.

"No more talking. You die. Here in this thread."

"Monte!" Sandy screamed.

Monte turned away from Paul. Something strange about his wife's voice, like she blubbered underwater. Rebecca watched them, looked at Alan and Ginny, looked at Sandy. She was close to losing her mind.

Sandy coughed and retched. Crystal clear water spouted from her nose and mouth. Water somehow soaked her clothes as if welling up from her skin. She couldn't breathe. Her eyes were wide and afraid.

"She drowns," Paul said. "After falling from a boat you pilot, Monte. You didn't notice she had fallen off until it was too late."

"Stop it!" Monte yelled, running to Sandy, trying in vain to shake her free from the attack. "In another thread I save her! Isn't that right?"

"True," Paul said.

"Bring her into that thread. Please!"

"She's an enemy in every thread, Monte. I'm sorry."

Sandy fell to the ground, sopping wet and struggling for air. Monte roared in fury, knowing he was helpless. Again he lunged at Paul. This time, Monte burst into flames.

"And you, Monte, get caught in a high rise fire."

Monte windmilled his arms, looking for escape.

"Not as quick as the others, and I'm sorry for the discomfort, but this is the quickest end for you."

Sandy was still. Monte collapsed into a corner, unconscious from the smoke. Flames continued to consume his body.

Rebecca looked from body to body, her eyes large with shock and fright. Slowly, she turned her gaze to Paul. His eyes calm and gentle.

"Finally."

She shook where she stood, her fists clenched hard.

"You can relax now," he said. "Sorry for the chaos, but it's a new world for us. The old ways are gone and you and I will have a special place in things to come. An exalted place. Trust me. Overcome your shock and fear and you'll see."

She ran her hands through her hair. Her jaw chattered. Her eyes went from staring at the dead to looking out beyond reality.

"Oh no," Paul said. "She's split. No, Dear. Come back to me. You are fragile, and you lose your mind in many threads, but I'll bring you back to where your mind is strong."

In seconds, her body relaxed.

"There she is. You're back!"

"No," she said. "I never left."

Paul looked uncertain for the first time. "Well, either way. We can begin."

"I can see."

"I knew you would."

"That's not what I mean," she said. "I can see the sphere. Where all time happens."

He looked worried.

"You're right," she said. "We accomplish so much together. Our children are beautiful."

He relaxed again. "Let's live it out."

"Only here, in this thread where I've made my home, you murdered my husband."

He frowned. "No—"

"I have the sight now."

She laughed as he tried hard to concentrate.

"It's a shame what that tornado did to you in that other thread. The thread close to this one."

"Rebecca!"

His body thrashed as small bursts of lightning flared from limb to limb.

"Threw you into an electric fence," she said, shaking her head. "So sad."

He reached out to her, his agonized face begging for mercy as his body fried.

"If your inner character had been more pure, you would realize the full potential of the awakening we've experienced."

The jolting stopped as if the electricity had been cut off, maybe by a blown transformer. His breathing was erratic. His clothes smoldered. He could only stare. Only moments to live.

"Only the vulgar try to marry the threads of time," she said.

The basement was quiet. She looked around at the dead, settling last on her late husband, Alan. Above came voices and the sounds of electric winches. Rescuers had come. In minutes they will unblock the entrance to the basement.

"The pure in heart can travel the threads. That's what I'll do. I'm going to be with Alan again. I have no interest in you."

He heard those words and died.

The screech of metal tore through the air. The door burst open, and rescuers galloped down the stairs and walked into the incredible scene. Had they been seconds earlier, they would have seen Rebecca vanish into the sphere of time.

James B. Christensen

Lake Pastora

A small item in the news caught my attention this morning. An outbreak in a big, riverfront city. Unexplainable. Officials alarmed but confident they will identify and defeat this new intruder.

I have a hunch what is happening. Several months have passed since the horror I witnessed. Long enough to let myself believe it might be over for good. Foolish me. I cannot bear to see how awful things will get. I know what came out of the river to afflict that metropolis so full of people because I know how it went in.

I was a freelance writer who earned my living traveling America to investigate the strange and unusual. I acquired a taste for it while in college when I traveled to the middle of Nebraska to write about a forest that supposedly contained a gateway to hell. It was fun to do and got me noticed. I wrote of unknown creatures and paranormal phenomena for local magazines, which led to bigger, more widely read publications. Soon, I made a decent living for a single man, driving my pickup across the country, seeing queer sights and meeting unique people.

While in Nebraska I had learned of small towns submerged by shifting rivers and man-made lakes. The ruins I viewed there were foundations of houses long consumed by the water, and the residents had plenty of time to move to dry land. Still, the subject fascinated me, and research led me to Lake Pastora. That small lake on the outskirts of the Black Hills had the granddaddy town-drowning story of them all. I sensed a payday and packed my bag.

It was just past lunchtime when I arrived at the lake. It sat just north of Torrence, South Dakota, where I filled my belly and asked for directions. There I was given a hand-drawn map and told to look for Harvey Finney. I found my way to the lake turn-off. My pickup shook and bounced along the poorly maintained county road, and it eventually leveled off as I curved around a wooded area. I followed signs until the lake came into view. I turned into a scenic overlook, got out of the pickup, and stared at the lake.

It was wide and round. Very large, but hardly a huge lake. At the lake's edge, opposite of where I stood, the land rose into the foothills of the Black Hills. An immense, natural wall bordered that side of the lake. A large fissure split its middle, forming a natural V. I felt a tingle of excitement, although looking back, maybe it was foreboding and I had just misidentified it.

Scanning the clearing, I spotted a dock stretching into the water from the lake's north edge. A small cabin sat just offshore. I assumed that was Mr. Finney's cabin. At the end of the dock was a small boat. That was my destination.

I returned to my pickup and doubled back to an earlier fork in the road and followed the outer path until signs appeared to guide me to the dock. I drove out of the woods and into the clearing that surrounded the lake. Harvey stepped out of his cabin when he heard the sound of my truck driving up and parking in the small meadow next to his cabin. He was a spry old man, tall and weatherworn with twinkling blue eyes and an ornery smile. He waved as I parked and stretched.

"How do you do, friend?" he asked.

"Very well, thanks," I said, shaking his hand. "Tony Garrity."

"Harvey Finney. You aren't lost, are you?"

"Just sightseeing," I said.

"She's a beauty," he said, sweeping his hands out toward the water.

I looked around. It was beautiful. "Yours the only cabin here?"

"'Fraid so," he said. "No fish in the lake, so no fishermen. No shore-line to speak of. The lake's edge drops straight down, so no swimmers."

I spotted No Fishing and No Swimming signs near the water.

"Campers?" I asked.

He shook his head. "A few. The woods are so thick, there ain't many clearings for a tent. No camping slots."

I nodded as I studied the mirror-like waters of the lake. Judging by Harvey's tone, he didn't lament the lack of tourists.

"So what brings you out here, Harvey?"

He smiled as if he got the question a lot. "Sentimental value. I was five when this lake was formed in 1947."

"The lake's that young, eh?"

"Would you like to have a look around?" Harvey asked. "I'll be happy to give you the tour."

We left in Harvey's four-wheel-drive Bronco. He navigated fast and sharp for a man his age, like someone who knew the twists and turns like the lines on his face.

He dropped the truck into low gear as we crawled up a steep road. I tried to hide my anxiety as we inched above the timberline. He didn't hide his amusement. When we leveled off, we were hundreds of feet higher, and I could see the lake and surrounding trees to our left. We were on a road that topped the high ridge I'd observed earlier. On our right was a wide basin, itself the size of a lake, but empty and desolate. The flat Dakota plains stretched off to the east beyond that.

Harvey eased the Bronco to the edge of a small suspension bridge that spanned the v-shaped fissure. He turned off the vehicle and let me look around.

"Holy cow," I said, in awe of the postcard-perfect view.

He flashed a wide grin of local pride at my wonderment.

"Never fails to take my breath away," he said.

We watched the lake in silence. From where we sat, the stillness of the lake was evident.

"Looks like glass," I said.

He lowered his gaze to the water. "Not much wind through there. Not sure why."

"You said the lake was formed in '47?"

He confirmed that with grin and a nod. "August 22."

"In one day?" I asked.

Harvey beamed at my astonishment.

"Well, Harvey, I hope you're gonna tell me the whole story."

"Take a look out there," he said, pointing to the flat, empty basin to our right.

"That used to be Lake Pastora," he said. "I remember it vaguely. Used to swim there."

I could tell he loved this part. I didn't mind a little showbiz.

Then he pointed to the left. "And the town of Torrance was over there."

"Where the lake is now?"

He nodded. "As you can see, the town sat lower than the old lake, but why worry? Only an act of God could break a natural barrier this high right?"

I waited, letting him tell his well-rehearsed tale.

"On August 22, 1947, at 4 a.m., a meteorite struck the west edge of the old Lake Pastora, creating this split right here in front of us. The impact set off a seismic event. The bedrock under Torrance sank fifty feet straight down, taking the entire town with it."

He grinned at my reaction. I had never heard of such a thing. I looked at the empty basin, back to the "new" Lake Pastora and did the math.

"I can see you're working it out, and you're right," he said. "The water poured out of the old lake through the crack in the hill and filled up the new hole, creating the new lake you see here."

"But the town? The people?"

"Like I said, it was four o'clock in the morning. I imagine they all woke up to the shaking, and came out to see fifty foot walls of earth all around them, with water gushing down."

"No way to get out?"

"I imagine they tried their best to crawl out, but the water poured in so fast . . ."

"How many people?"

"Three hundred, sixty-eight people unaccounted for." He looked away. "Including my parents."

I kept a respectful silence for a few seconds.

"I'm damn sorry to hear that, Harvey."

"Thank you. I hope it was fast for them. Either way, drowning's not a nice way to go."

I stared at the lake, now understanding why there was no fish, no swimming, no camping. It was a mass water grave. A chilly, unsettling vibe radiated out from the waters. I realized then I hadn't seen or heard a bird or any other form of animal life. Who would want to stay here?

"Sentimental value, eh?" I asked.

He nodded. "I was one of a few to survive. The lucky ones, like me, were out of town when it happened. I was staying with my grandparents in Huron. The decision was made to start over, and now the new town of Torrence sits a half-mile behind us."

I took a deep breath, wondering what I should do or say next.

"Has anyone ever told your story?"

"Told my story?"

"Yeah, you know, like in a magazine or newspaper?"

"No. Never have."

"I'll do it if you don't mind."

"You a reporter?"

"Sort of."

"So you didn't come here by accident, did you?"

"All I knew was that Torrence had an interesting story, but I had no idea."

He chuckled. "As long as you don't make me out a fool, I don't mind."

"I promise."

We eased across the suspension bridge and my stomach fluttered.

"Well, if you're gonna make me famous," he said. "I've got one more thing to show you."

"There's more?"

"You're gonna love this."

We returned to his cabin, and he led me out to the dock I noticed when I drove in. As we walked toward the edge, I realized it wasn't a boat waiting at the end. A small yellow tower bobbed in the water.

"Is that a—"

"Submarine? Yes," Harvey said, very proud to say the word.

"I'll be damned. A yellow submarine, even."

"Sorry?"

"You know, yellow submarine?"

Harvey didn't get it.

"It's a nice color."

"I can take eight people at a time," he said. "Rarely have that many, though."

I was anxious to get in, having never been in a submarine before. Harvey watched me. He made no move to enter the submarine or invite me in. Whatever ball was in play had dropped on my side of the net. Then it hit me.

"Oh, uh, how much for the ride?"

"Twenty dollars for thirty minutes. I promise you it's money well spent."

I wasn't sure at first if it sounded like a good deal, but I remembered what lie at the bottom of the lake. I fished out a twenty and handed it to him. He opened the hatch of the submarine tower and we crawled in.

It was comfortable and clean, with a bright, white interior. Four porthole windows lined either side of the vessel. I settled into one of the soft passenger seats as Harvey sat in the pilot seat in the center of a large bubble at the submarine's forward end. He started the engine, and I felt a ripple of childish excitement as we descended into the murky depths.

I glanced out my porthole window and saw nothing. I checked the other windows, and they were dark, too.

"Hold on," he said, reading my mind.

He switched out the outer lights. I could see the earthen wall of the lake on our right as we descended. Only bits of moss and other floating particles were visible to the left. There were no fish.

"Just hold your horses, Tony," he said. "We'll be upon it soon."

Soft, classical piano came from the overhead speakers.

"Doin' all right?" he asked.

"Just fine. How long have you been doing these tours?"

"A little over ten years now. I put in forty years with the railroad. Never married, so I had plenty of money to spend."

I opened my pocket notebook and wrote out a few details.

"Here we are," he said.

I put away the notebook and looked out my porthole window. The submarine lights flashed three times, and I worried that something was wrong. I watched Harvey, but he flipped a switch, and the lights stayed on. He looked unconcerned, so I didn't worry.

A gas station appeared first, appearing out of the murk and into the bright submarine lights. Ray's Philips 66, the sign said. Gas for fifteen cents a gallon. An old Ford pickup sat askew near a pump, giving a sign of the town's violent end.

Harvey was silent as we traversed the small town streets, passing a grocery store, a lawyer's office, diners, and doctor's offices. Buildings lined the ghostly street on either side of us. The sub floated eye-level with the second floors of the buildings. I tried to imagine how we must have looked, the submarine floating through the deserted streets like a spaceship exploring a lost and forgotten world.

The submarine turned down another street, and we sailed over a city park like we were on a Sunday drive. The metal frames of park benches sat empty amongst the thick, barren trees. We went past a small school. Abandoned playground equipment sat in an overgrown field. I imagined a town this small likely hosted students of every grade in this building. At four a.m., the time of the disaster, the building was empty, as were all the businesses.

Harvey maneuvered the sub through the streets, over ball fields and around a small factory. We passed a small police station. A Chevrolet police car sat out front. Next door was a shoe store. I watched it all sail by in spellbound wonder.

I got queasy when we turned into the residential areas. When the town settled and flooded, everyone would have been in their homes. This had been a pre-24/7 world. The town had gone to sleep and awakened to apocalyptic terror only to go back to sleep forever.

Cars were in the driveway. Toys in the yards. The grass had grown to eerie heights and undulated in the current. Harvey slowed the sub to a halt in front of a Victorian home that looked old even for this setting. He stared at this house without speaking. I waited until I was uncomfortable.

"My house," he said, sensing my restlessness.

I nodded and realized there was one thing I hadn't seen. One thing that, should I write this story, people would wonder about. I looked at Harvey's childhood home again, in the spotlights underwater, and knew their bones lay somewhere within its walls.

"Say, Harvey . . . I hate to ask about this, and I mean no disrespect —"

"I've never seen any bodies," he said.

He didn't sound offended.

"You'd think there'd be a skeleton or two," he said. "Everything happened so fast, but still, some of them must have made it out of their homes to try to get away."

"Was there a rescue effort?"

Harvey shook his head. "Didn't have the resources in those days. Besides, when nobody came up for air on the first day, it was obvious they never would."

"What about recovering the bodies for burial?"

"It was talked about, but no one had the stomach for it. The relatives of the lost decided to let the lake be their resting place. A minister performed a service and blessed the water."

"Did anyone float to the surface?"

"No."

That surprised me.

Harvey moved the sub forward, and the tour continued. Despite the grim history, I was still in awe of that underwater time capsule. My morbid curiosity overwhelmed my good taste, and I stared hard into the windows and storefronts, looking for a skeletal hand or a grinning skull. I spotted occasional debris here and there—boxes, furniture, books, shoes. But there was no sign of the dead other than their abandoned homes and businesses.

A low rumble sounded from below, and a sudden current spun the submarine 180 degrees.

"Whoa!" Harvey said, looking surprised.

His hands flashed across the levers and switches, and he brought the vessel under control again before it hit a street light. He looked back at me with a nervous grin.

"You okay?"

I must have looked a wreck. My hands had a white-knuckle grip on the armrests of my chair.

"Fine," I said, short of breath. "What happened?"

"Can't say for sure."

"Has that ever happened before?"

"No."

He went back to piloting the sub as if nothing had gone wrong. Since he wasn't worried, I tried to relax. Pride stopped me from demanding he return us to the surface at once. I concentrated on the soothing music and watched as he concluded the tour. At the end of town, he raised the sub above the rooftops and took us back toward the dock. I looked at old Torrance from above as it faded from view and returned to the inky gloom beneath us. I exhaled when we returned to the sunlight and fresh air.

I waited on the dock as Harvey secured the vessel and closed it up. He grinned at me and gave me a friendly slap on the back.

"What'd ya think?"

"That was amazing!"

I worried that my enthusiasm was disrespectful to his loss, but he seemed thrilled I had enjoyed the tour.

"Do you get a lot of business?" I asked.

"Not much. I don't advertise. I take people out as they find me. Most days I go alone."

"Well, I appreciate this, Harvey. This could be the most interesting story I've ever written."

"I can't wait to read all about it!"

We stood in silence for a few seconds. I surveyed the thick woods surrounding the lake. A small tent now sat a short distance from Harvey's cabin. A college-age couple busied themselves setting up camp. Colorado plates tagged their Honda. They weren't far from the No Swimming and No Fishing signs, so their plans were likely as simple as enjoying nature for the day and enjoying each other through the night.

"Looks like you have customers," I said to Harvey.

He didn't answer. I looked at him and caught him frowning as he watched the lake.

"Harvey? Everything all right?"

He snapped out of it. "Huh? Oh, yes. Sorry."

He saw the campers.

"Oh, right. Campers. I'd better go say hello."

I watched him walk over to the couple. I turned to study the water, trying to figure out what had Harvey concerned. As it had been since I arrived, the water was still, only rippling a little from our trip. I didn't know the lake well enough to know the water level had dropped six feet.

The experience of the underwater tour, and Harvey's tragic connection to the disaster had me in a mood to get back to Torrance and write my story. There was a motel and a bed-and-breakfast somewhere. Harvey, returned from meeting the couple and invited me to stay with him for the night. He had two spare rooms in his cabin, and it was a cozy and rustic place. The promise of premium beer sealed the deal.

The camping couple joined us for dinner. Harvey grilled hamburgers for everyone. Tyler and Alisha, the couple, were friendly and good-humored. Three years into their marriage, they were in the middle of a random road trip, stopping and camping wherever they found something that caught their fancy. Tyler kept glancing at Alisha. I could tell he wanted to get her back to the tent and all to himself. They turned in early and Harvey and I exchanged a grinning look.

We turned in not long after. I settled into bed under a pile of quilts and spent a few minutes outlining the frame of my story, then shut off the lamp and drifted off in absolute silence and darkness.

If only the story had ended there. If only I had followed my instincts and left at dusk.

I woke from a heavy sleep the next morning. The darkness held me in its thrall throughout the night, a welcome relief from my normal disruptive sleep pattern. I stepped outside to breathe the fresh lake air. There was only a hint of sunrise. The lake was a wide, round shadow. The trees silhouetted against the faint sunrise like shark's teeth. A heavy morning mist clouded the air. Water beaded up on my face and arms. Each breath brought tiny droplets of water into my nose, tickling as they went.

My muscles and joints enjoyed a hearty stretch. I glanced over to Tyler and Alisha's tent and lost my breath. Last night it had stood tall and tight. Now it was a flat, rumpled pile of nylon fabric and broken tent poles. Their Honda sat in the same place.

Unsure if it was an emergency or not, I didn't wake Harvey when I ran back into his cabin to finish dressing. I had slept in my clothes, so I only had to throw on my shoes. I jogged the fifty yards to their campsite, slowing to a walk as I drew closer. Sunrise came rapidly. I looked around for any sign of them cooking breakfast, hiking, something.

Their light blue Honda glistened with a mossy green slime. I didn't know what to make of that. Either way, I was putting off what I knew I had to do—check under the collapsed tent.

I took a breath, stood as far away as I could and still reach, and eased the tent fabric away. First, I saw a foot—feminine judging by the pink toenail polish, but barely human. The skin was bone-white, the flesh shriveled and hugging the bone as if everything but skin and bones had been sucked away.

I felt dizzy. I should have fled, but felt an obligation to at least check and see if they were still alive. I tossed the tent open and the sight and smell of what was once Tyler and Alisha assaulted my senses. My stomach cramped, but I held down the heaves. The rest of them was as

Alisha's foot had been. Both naked. Their eyes sunken and their hair a stringy mess. Their mouths were wide open in screams that went unheard by Harvey and I. That or they suffered their fate too fast for sound to escape.

The bodies and the interior of the tent were awash in the odd slime I found on their car.

I dropped the tent and stood up, catching my breath. There was nothing left but to summon the county sheriff. I stared at the young couple in shock. I had never seen dead bodies before. It was a hell of a first time.

"They crave blood. Mostly for moisture."

Harvey's voice frightened me so badly I jumped into the air and landed facing him.

"Jesus, Harvey! You scared the hell out of me."

"Sorry."

Then it dawned on me what he'd said.

"What do you mean? Did you say *they* crave blood?"

He shrugged, looking embarrassed. "I didn't say anything because I didn't think it would be a problem."

"A problem? These people are dead! Human beings!"

I collected my thoughts, trying to come to grips that what happened to Tyler and Alisha hadn't come as a surprise to Harvey.

"What happened here?" I asked.

"They must've crawled out in the night after the lake drained away."

"I don't understand."

Now it was Harvey's turn to look astonished.

"You didn't see the lake this morning? For Christ's sake, Tony, how did you miss it?"

It was too dark for me to have noticed when I left the cabin, but in the metallic blue of early morning, everything was visible. I looked at the lake and uttered one befuddled profanity after another.

There was no water. Lake Pastora yesterday. Giant hole in the earth today.

Harvey and I jogged to the rim and looked into the empty lake. In the center, the dripping and rotted buildings of old Torrance sparkled wet in the rising sun. The tall grass flopped over wet on its side. There were cars and shattered glass and empty, broken streets. A ghost town given up by the waters that kept it hidden.

"Remember that shaking we felt when we were in the sub?" Harvey asked.

I backed away from him. He was forty-odd years older than me, but I sensed I was in danger.

"I remember," I said. "And the sudden current."

"Must've been an earthquake. Opened a fissure along the lake bed."

"Where's the water now?"

Another shrug. "Underground, I guess."

I pointed to the wrecked tent. "And what does this have to do with that?"

"I think it's aliens myself."

I walked around him, back toward the cabin.

"I'm leaving, Harvey. And I'm calling the sheriff."

"I'm not joking, Tony. I think it was an organism or cells on that '47 meteorite that caused all this. Something that got into the people underwater."

I stopped and turned to face him.

"When they drowned, the organisms got inside, changed them," he said. "Kept them alive, but not alive."

"Are you on medication, Harvey?"

"A smart-ass thing to say considering what you see around you."

He had a point.

"How do you know this?"

He took a deep breath. "I found my parents. It was way past when anyone could be alive, but I wanted to get them a proper burial. I learned to dive and searched around."

"And you found them?"

"They found me," he said. "Not just mom and dad, but dozens of them, coming out of houses and such. Most of them I recognized. I was on a dive, and it was all I could do to get away. I came back with rope and dragged mom and dad up and free from the lake. They attacked me, but I got the better of 'em."

"What happened to your parents?"

"Died for good."

"How?"

"I buried them. Behind the cabin a piece. They're at rest."

"And the others?"

"They stay hidden. I flash my sub lights to let them know I'm coming. All was well and would've stayed well if the lake hadn't drained."

"You should have told someone."

"I'm sorry about those two youngsters. I didn't know this would happen. Honest."

"I believe you. And nobody will blame you for this, Harvey. But we've got to tell the sheriff. I'm leaving."

I turned and walked to the cabin. I heard a metallic click.

"Stop walking, Tony."

Long fingers of sunlight descended through the trees as the sun continued to rise. It reflected off the barrel of Harvey's gun when I turned to face him. I was scared, but getting shot was preferable to what happened to Tyler and Alisha.

"So how does this end for me, Harvey?"

"It'll end good if you promise to keep your mouth shut."

I looked around at the incredible scene. The empty lake. The rotted ruins of Torrance. The dead couple. Harvey and his gun. I noticed something new. At the lake rim were gouges and claw marks in the mud. Wet, dragging footprints, several across, tracked from the lake, between Harvey and I, and away in the direction of new Torrance.

"How many are there?"

"Hundreds."

"Where are they now?"

"On their way to Torrance by the aim of those tracks."

"There's a danger here," I said. "To the people of Torrance."

"Oh, I'm counting on it."

I couldn't believe it. "You want this to happen?"

"You keep saying I should've told someone. Well, I did. Tried to get help and make people listen and explore the lake. Got me a psychiatric evaluation and my name made into a laughingstock for my trouble."

"They'll believe you now."

"Damn right they will," he said. "Now, if you promise to get the hell outta Dodge and keep your mouth shut, I'll let you go."

I agreed. What choice did I have? I could always break such a ridiculous oath later. For now, it was a way out. I turned carefully, not wanting to spook him, to return to the cabin and get my things. My argument with Harvey kept me from noticing that a new wave of creatures had crawled from the lake. They stood in a row between me and the cabin, twenty or more strong.

Their soaked and tattered clothes reeked in the mountain air. Hair hung like wet mops. Their bodies were plump and gorged. Teeth were unnaturally long. All the better to drain their victims, I supposed. They stared at me through cloudy, enlarged eyes. First one, then the others took tentative steps in my direction. Comfortable of their footing, they walked fast. Much too fast for my comfort.

Slapping sounds at the lake's rim caught my attention. I stole a quick look and saw webbed human hands clawing at the mud. More creatures came into view as their hideous faces peeked over the rim.

"Better run for it, Son," Harvey said. "They're faster than you'd think. You'll never outrun 'em to your truck."

I took off in a sprint toward the trees, perpendicular from where the tracks led.

"That's good, don't go toward Torrence!" he yelled after me. "Not a pleasant place to be right now, I'll bet!"

He punctuated that last comment with a cackle that chilled my blood and echoed off the trees, following me into the darkness of the woods.

I was not and have never been a sprinter or a long-distance runner. At first, I outran the staggering creatures, but as I tired, they caught up. I heard them grunting and calling out to me or each other with an odd, guttural yodel. Their pace did not relent, and as I slowed, they drew closer.

After an eternity I burst free of the woods and onto a flat prairie. I didn't know if this favored me or them, but I found new energy and ran faster. There were no farms or country gas stations. No signs of life anywhere. By then I ran on pure instinct, using every ounce of energy to survive until there was no more.

A stabbing ache flashed through my side. My lungs burned. I didn't have much strength left. I considered what to do. To collapse without the strength to fight the beasts as they ravaged me was an unappealing idea. To save muscle power for when all was lost was also a no-go. In my desperation, I tried to think of ways I could kill myself here in the middle of nowhere. A sharp stick to the neck, maybe.

I slowed to a walk, grabbing my side, catching my breath. One of the creatures, bald and fat, wearing an old-fashioned, three-piece suit fell forward onto his face. He gasped and thrashed in the dirt, letting loose with an almost-human scream. It was so awful a sound I had pity on the thing. First one, then another, then all of them dropped to the dirt, likewise screaming and thrashing until all were still and quiet. I had survived. There, standing in the prairie grass surrounded by dead mutants, I wondered what came next.

What came next was Harvey's navy Ford Bronco speeding through field. He wove around my pursuers so as not to "kill" any of them. Here to shoot me, no doubt. Let him. I was too tired to run. He slid to a stop in front of me. I waited for my bullet.

"Get in, dammit," he said.

With no argument, I got into the Bronco and sighed with relief as he sped away. He looked at the dead things and I saw sadness in his face.

"Like I said, they need the moisture. That's why they attack. They need the blood. Any wet fluid we got. Without it . . ."

He jerked his thumb at the bodies.

"The lake water kept 'em happy. Kept 'em controlled."

The Bronco bounced through a ditch and onto a gravel road. I could see the forest surrounding Lake Pastora coming close and knew that was our destination.

"What now, Harvey?"

"Gonna get you out of here," he said. "I was thinkin' about it. I've got scores to settle, but you ain't a part of it. Dammit, I like you, Tony."

I said nothing. I was off the hook and wasn't about to run my mouth. Harvey took us back to his cabin through a little-used road. More tracks led out of the lake toward Torrance.

"Go on," he said. "Get your stuff and get out of here."

I ran into the cabin and to my room. I kept looking over my shoulder as I threw my belongings into my bag. Thank God I traveled light.

I came out of the cabin to see Harvey loading the last of eight large Coleman coolers into the back of his Bronco. Nothing was said as he finished his loading and each of us got behind our steering wheels.

"Like I said, do not go through Torrence or you won't get out. You go around the lake to the west, see?" he said, pointing. "Past that boulder is a road that'll take you to a county road. Take it straight west and you'll hit the interstate. You're on your own from there. You'll keep your promise to stay quiet?"

I nodded, thinking that somehow made it less of a promise.

He put his car in gear and rolled forward.

"Harvey?"

I couldn't resist one question. He stopped and looked at me.

"What are you going to do?"

He grinned and jerked his thumb at the coolers behind him.

"Ice from the lake," he said. "I've got a chunk for every major river and a few for the oceans. Going on a road trip."

My face went pale. It pleased him.

"That's right, Tony. The world didn't care about me. Now I'm settin' fire to it."

I stuttered to tell him all the ways his vile plan wouldn't work. He chuckled.

"The earthquake already drained the lake into the groundwater," he said. "I'm just adding frosting to the cake."

I knew there was no stopping him.

"Boil your water before cooking or drinking," he said.

With those bizarre parting words, he drove away. I followed his instructions and drove around the lake's edge to the hidden exit. I studied the ruins of old Torrance as I circled the lake. The ruins were empty. No more former residents making their way to the edge to climb up. I almost lost control, so I fixed my eyes on the road before I drove into the chasm and sealed my fate.

So I escaped, more or less. Several months it's been since I watched Harvey drive away on his awful errand. The news of the aquatic creatures attacking swimmers in a lakefront big city is confirmation that Harvey met with success. He tossed his ice chunks into the river where they melted and set free the alien organism, no doubt. If his health held up, he tossed them into other rivers and God forbid, the Atlantic and Pacific oceans.

I moved to an acreage far from Lake Pastora. The property's water comes from a well that careful research told me was far from any aquifer near the cursed lake. I collect rainwater and boil any water that didn't come from the sky or my well. I grow my food and have learned to live off the land and keep to myself, going into the nearest town for books and supplies and whatever I cannot provide for myself.

A pool sits behind my cabin. It looks amusingly out of place, but I need water. Several heavy spring rains filled up the pool. I keep the filter clean. It's funny, but water, once the source of my mortal fear, has become my ally and protector. I spend my free time floating in the water. When it rains, I walk in it. In the wintertime, I keep my tub heated and full.

At first, I figured this infatuation with water was my way of facing and conquering my fear. The day I realized water had become an unnatural need was one of dark realization. Small, fleshy webbing appeared between my fingers and toes one morning. My incisors developed a sharpness that I dismissed as natural at first but they are unnaturally long now. My eyesight changes by the day, fading from normal sight yet awakening to new vistas once unseeable.

I'm not sure how the organism entered my body. I never swam in the lake nor drank its water. My guess is that the thick mist the morning I discovered the dead couple is the culprit. I harbor no resentment. I am now more than human. There will be more of us. I journey into town and into the big cities to swim in their pools and rivers and lakes and watch them drink from jugs and fountains and I grin to myself.

It's funny, I lived for months after Lake Pastora fearing the wet slapping of mutant hands at my windows. But the invasion came from within. There was nothing to fear. Soon I'll make my way to the mighty rivers and the oceans beyond. The world is three-fourths water, and there will be plenty of room for me and my newfound brethren.

There will be plenty of room for you, too.

Life of Luxury

Janet McGee woke early with the sun. Wide beams of solar warmth filled the vast master bedroom. Her eyes fluttered open then closed against the brightness. For a moment, she hid herself behind closed eyes, in a timeless world of thought and imagination. She had risen from sleep on a day of reckoning. There was no hiding from decisions made in the past. Accounts would be weighed today. A day for comparison. What might have been versus what will be.

She sat up, opening her eyes again as her head entered a strip of shadow. She looked out the French doors—left open overnight to enjoy the fresh, fall cool—past the bedroom terrace and out to the far mountain range and the fat sun rising over it. The look of the sun at this time of year reminded her of the butterscotch candies her father used to give her when she was a child. She missed him a lot. In older days, there had been no terrace. No mountain range. Only a filthy window kept shut against city noise. The only view the brick wall of the neighboring tenement.

She turned away from the outdoors to watch her husband, Merle, as he slept. He was peaceful, his breathing steady and his face relaxed. She had slept soundly, which surprised her. There was a time when sleep was interrupted by car horns and screams, when she felt Merle toss and turn throughout the night. When she staggered out of bed feeling as though she'd had no rest at all.

The sun was so warm and the air so perfect she considered returning to her pillow for another hour or two of rest, but she decided against it.

She wanted to make today of all days count for as much as she could add to it—a refreshing change from when all she wanted to do was hide from the day in any way possible.

Her feet touched the champagne-colored silk carpet. Its softness and warmth caressed her toes and she had a fleeting thought she might spend the day running her feet through it. Perhaps lie naked and roll about and flutter her arms and legs as if making a snow angel. She thought of the little things and wondered if that was the key to the mind of the rich. The little things. Even her feet looked better than ever. Pampered and polished. Gone were the calluses and crusty heels. Gone were the thick thermal socks she once wore to keep her feet warm. Also gone where her pitiful attempts to paint her own toes in the manner of the women in the fashion magazines she saw in the library. Even Merle noticed, for sure. Her feet were as soft as the silk carpet.

The tiles on the outdoor terrace cooled her soles. An arousing tingle traveled through her calves at the change of temperature. She walked to the stone balustrade and rested her hands upon it. An early-fall breeze greeted her arrival, and she turned her face into it. It fluttered her ivory silk pajamas, and she smiled. Despite the potential for anxiety today, she was at peace. There was no smog in the air, no stench of urine and exhaust. The air was so crystal clear she nearly wept at its purity.

A pair of large strong hands caressed her waist and gently explored. Merle kissed the side of her neck. She turned to him and grinned.

"Mornin', Hon," he said.

"Hi."

His hands ran up her pajama top. He touched her all the time now. They stared at the rising sun together.

"What're them mountains called again?" she asked.

He frowned, trying to remember.

"Uhhh. The Radials? The Royals? I ain't sure."

"They already told us what they was," she said. "But I'd be too embarrassed to ask again."

"Doesn't matter now, I guess."

She reached behind to do some caressing of her own. Once there was an invisible barrier between them. A ghostly wall that made intimacy impossible, a laughable idea. That barrier vanished when they moved here.

"What should we do with our day?"

"Gonna be a busy night," he said.

"Yeah, I know," she said, her smile narrowing. "But today it's just us."

"I say we screw." He kissed her. "And then we screw again." Another kiss.

Was it anxiety that had him so amorous? The sex was good and plentiful since their sudden success.

"We been doin' it a lot," she said. "Anything else you want to do?"

"I feel like I should be tired when we have our thing tonight. Know what I mean? Would seem ungrateful to show up otherwise. I could go runnin', or do a shit-ton of jumpin' jacks, or . . ."

After making love on the terrace, they moved into the master bathroom.

"This bathroom is bigger'n our old living room," Merle said. "Remember?"

That old bathroom was so filthy she hated to use it. She hurried in and out. The toilet was gross. The shower weak and depressing. Here, the heated floor kept her feet warm.

Pampered feet. The symbol of success she didn't know about until she had it.

"And them sinks are bigger than our kitchen table," she said.

Merle entered the closet-sized shower and turned gold-plated knobs until the shower and hydro-spa heads running along and above the stall hissed to life. He smiled and waved her in. His calm still mystified her. She entered and felt the sharp prickle of hot water. After another couple rounds of lovemaking, they washed up and dried their bodies.

While toweling off each other's bodies, they decided a horseback ride across the seventy acres of lush lawn and forest was the best way to pass most of the morning and afternoon. After a hearty breakfast, they ventured out to the stables and found the stable hands were ready and helpful. They set out in the high noon sun at a trot. They glanced at each other as they approached the woods. In their eyes each saw the flash of possibility of galloping off the estate and trying their best to disappear. She held his look, knowing his thoughts and waiting to see what he would do. He winked and rode on. She smiled and followed. It was the right decision. There was no disappearing from their new friends.

Their ride took them across the breadth and width of the estate. They ascended a ridge that afforded them a view of the palace—50,000 square feet of stone, glass, and marble. Absolute heaven on earth. Behind them stood the mountains they could not name.

"I guess we'd ought to ask ourselves if it was worth it," Merle said.

She nodded, not wanting to discuss it, but knowing it was a conversation they had to have today.

"I think so," she said.

"I ain't sure 'I think so' is enough," he said. "I feel responsible."

"You are. But in a good way. Not the bad way. You gave me all of this. Where we lived before? I couldn't walk the streets in the daytime. Now look at us."

"But was that better than this? You know, considerin' what we traded for it?"

She laughed. "Better'n this? Merle, during our marriage I had to make three trips to the hospital after you'd tried to kill yourself."

Merle looked away.

"We're lucky Mr. Melton found us. Made us this offer."

"My mama would've said we traded one weight for another."

"Your mama died poor and alone, Hon."

He nodded. "You're right. We made our choice, and I've loved it all."

"It's late afternoon," she said. "Let's go have lunch."

"And a nap?" he said with a wink.

They rode back to the palace and lunch was waiting. They took their time, ordering more courses and desserts. All of it delivered without a hint of disapproval from the staff.

After lunch, they huddled together in the cinema and watched two films. They returned to their bedroom for "nap time" without sleeping. Janet was amazed at Merle's staying power. Always ready, always able to perform on demand and for as long as she needed. In the old days, both felt fat and ugly and blamed each other for it.

"The sun is low," he said.

The early evening shadows fell across them as they lay tangled on the messed up king-sized bed.

"Won't be long now," she said. "Have you thought about it much?"

"I'm kind of excited about it," he said. "That's what I'm trainin' my mind to think, anyway."

"Really?"

"Everything's different for people who live like this. Even the final step is different. We all got to go there sooner or later. This beats what was waitin' for us back home in the old life."

"Yeah. I guess so."

"How about another shower?"

"You mean a fun shower?"

"Everything's fun here."

After a second session of sex-and-shower, they walked naked into the walk-in closet. It was walled with mirrors and a small bar divided the his and hers sections. Their cramped old closet was only a few feet wide, which was adequate because they had few clothes.

Merle poured himself a finger of scotch from a crystal decanter.

"Go easy on that, Merle. We're supposed to go easy on the booze today."

A look of apprehension flickered across his face and left. The first sign of fear she had seen from him in weeks. It was time to dress for the evening. Maybe the finality of it was upon him. He nodded.

"Yeah, I know. I'll be fine. Just don't want to let anymore go to waste than I have to."

"I remember when Mogen David was your booze of choice," she said.

He frowned. "Why you jawin' so much about the old days?"

"Ain't it obvious?"

He swallowed his drink. "Maybe we shouldn't make it so obvious."

"Okay."

"I've turned my ass to the old days. I'm good."

"Okay, Merle."

A row of suits and other men's clothes lined his side of the closet. He rummaged through them—a little rough considering how fine the tailor-made threads were, she thought—and chose a pewter-colored suit and white shirt. He selected a tie with sapphire ocean waves. Not once, she noticed, did he give a single look at his naked body, even though every wall was a floor-to-ceiling mirror.

She looked away from him to her own reflection. Her hair had been gray when they'd moved into Wintergate Palace. Now it was black as a raven's beak. Her fingernails, once chewed to the quick, were long and polished and set with diamonds. Real ones, she would brag if she saw her old friends and family. Her breasts were large and perky in her prime, but they had relented to gravity. Now they were full and at attention again. A tummy tuck had removed the saggy paunch. A personal trainer had put her through the paces until her thighs and ass were worthy of a sculptor's admiration. Her wide, pug nose had been fixed. Not much could be done with her rough facial skin. In the old days, she was average for a woman in her mid-fifties. Now, she was a ten-percenter. How she wished she could show it off to the folks back home. To everyone. Old bosses, catty coworkers, uppity bitches from high school. She would stroll naked through town and school and the old grocery store and dare people to look away. She nodded to herself. Yes, I would do it. But the deal she and Merle had made wouldn't allow it. She was better than anyone in her past. Comfort in that knowledge was the best she could hope for. It would have to do only for the rest of the night.

"You should wear that today," Merle said.

He laced his wingtips.

"Just go in your birthday suit."

"There ain't no one here I want to impress other'n you," she said.

She didn't have to cycle through the endless selection of dresses in her closet. Today's dress had been chosen for her. It was a combination of black velvet and red silk, custom made and fitted for her form to show all that she had. It hugged what needed hugging and revealed what needed revealing. No undergarments. On it went. She got it arranged and zipped.

The mirror returned an agreeable reflection. She turned to see Merle admiring her.

"Real nice," he said.

"You look good, too," she said.

They watched each other in silence. Both of them smiling, trying not to break the spell, afraid of what lie behind their happy faces.

"I need to get my hair done," she said. "Meet you in the grand hall?"

"Sure, but don't be too long. They'll be here soon."

They went their separate ways. He didn't say it, but she knew he was going to the smoking room for another cigar. His preferred smoke per cigar cost more than their monthly rent in the old days. It was no worry though. He had two or three per day. He used to pour their limited money into those awful Camel non-filters. But she knew a man had a right to his smoke, and she was glad he had his indulgence.

The salon was in the master wing of the mansion, and Dorie waited for her. It was a relaxing time as her hair, hands, and feet were done. She stood admiring Dorie's efforts in the mirror.

"It's been an honor serving you, Ma'am," Dorie said.

Janet gave her a sharp glance. Not for speaking, but for the subtle reference to what was coming. Dorie stared at the floor, afraid.

"You've done a great job, Dorie," she said. "I would miss you but..."

Dorie kept her eyes on the Italian tile. "Yes, Ma'am."

The entertainment wing was on the opposite side of the mansion, and Janet had a long walk to get there. Not wanting to hurry, but mindful of the time, she slowed just enough to savor the sights as she passed. The massive library, the priceless works of art. The grand windows, each looking out to different natural beauties. The mahogany furniture. Mountains and mountains of money poured into this place. Riches beyond her imagination.

She passed the main entrance in time to see long stretch limousines arriving. She hurried to the lounge where she found Merle nursing another scotch. They kissed. Both were jumpy and full of energy.

"I'm curious to know how it ends," she said.

He frowned. "Are you nuts? Don't bring that up now. They'll be here any minute."

"I know, but I've been trying not to think about it and now that it's so close, I can't get it out of my mind."

"It's not for us to even wonder. Be thankful. That's our mindset. Be thankful."

"Thankful."

"Right."

A tuxedoed valet entered and announced:

"Mr. Jonathan Melton."

They stood at attention as the tall, elegant Mr. Melton entered the room. His aristocratic kindness put them at ease.

"My wonderful friends, the McGees," he said.

He received a kiss on the cheek from Janet and gave Merle a hearty handshake.

"So tell me," Mr. Melton said. "It's been a year since we last spoke. How do you like it here at Wintergate Palace?"

He said the last two words with such grandeur they expected his voice to echo off the walls. They answered his question with rapid-fire, *gee golly gosh* gushing about the mansion's splendor and luxury. He smiled with bemusement, but there was no condescension in his reaction. Still, Janet picked up on the fact that they were harped about extravagance that was mere trifle to him. She calmed and shot Merle a look that told him to be cool. Mr. Melton nodded understanding in the awkward silence.

"It is a glorious place," he said. "And I'm glad you found such joy here. That is very important."

"Mr. Melton, thank you for your kindness to us," Janet said.

"It's been my pleasure."

"Can I ask you a question?"

"Anything."

"Why us?"

He looked from Janet to Merle and back again. "I can sense your gratitude. A man who ascends to my heights learns a thing or two about humanity. Even in the depths were I found you, I knew you were people of gratitude."

"You never said how you found us," Merle said.

"Another benefit for a man of my station is access to whatever information I want and need, whenever I want it. I am always on the lookout for people such as yourselves. People at the end of their rope. People likely to show the greatest gratitude, and willing to trade up from their circumstances."

"You asked for a lot," Janet said with a nervous chuckle.

Mr. Melton smiled. He wasn't offended. "And I offered a lot in return, yes?"

"You sure did," Merle said.

"Material comforts. A life free of worry," Mr. Melton said. "And if history is any guide, you reached heights of passion you never thought possible. If you don't mind my saying."

The McGees looked at each other and laughed.

"Not only do I know people, I know the world. And when I say 'world' I also mean the worlds between the world. You see, it was long thought by my ancestors that terror and pain were the best way to appease the spirits that surround us and grant us their favor."

Janet and Merle felt a flash of apprehension, but Mr. Melton was so jovial in the way he spoke they let it pass.

"You've felt them, surely?" Mr. Melton asked.

"Who? The spirits?" Janet asked.

"Of course."

"Um . . ."

"In the woods. In the sunlight that rests upon you. When your bodies are joined?"

"Yeah, I guess so," Merle said.

"Our patron is as thirsty as any spirit or god throughout history. But she is a god of kindness. She wants the willing. She wants her sacrifice to be an act of love. For many decades now, I have had great success finding people of gratitude and love. Such as yourselves."

They masked their confusion with nods and smiles of agreement.

The valet returned and announced another arrival. A middle-aged couple—well-bred and rich—entered the lounge to greetings from Mr. Melton. He introduced them to the McGees, and the rich couple treated them with respect and interest. Janet, despite the improvements to her body and dress, still felt as though she stood out like a Christmas tree on Halloween. However, the couple credibly ignored the class gulf between them.

More couples arrived. Each one looking more refined and elegant than the last. When six couples had arrived, the valet shut the large oak doors to the lounge. They enjoyed finger foods and more expensive liquor. The night passed. The McGees felt at ease by everyone's friendliness.

An imposing grandfather clock near the fireplace rang out a mournful chime that brought all conversation to a halt. Everyone's face changed from carefree fun to sober seriousness of purpose.

Janet's breathing quickened. She took Merle's hand. Mr. Melton stood before them.

"And now, my friends, your end of the bargain comes due," he said.

One of the guests walked to a bookshelf and—in a move straight out of an old horror movie—removed a book that triggered a section of bookshelf to swing open, revealing a hidden passage. One by one the guests filed into the passage.

"When you hear the ring of the bell within," Mr. Melton said. "Join us."

He was the last to enter and disappear into the passage.

Alone in the lounge, Merle finished his drink. Janet shook, nervous.

"Come on, Babe," he said, hugging her. "We made the right choice. Let's not ruin it by being scared."

"I think I am scared."

"Fight it," he said. "Being afraid means we made the bum choice. Is that what you think?"

"No," she said.

He looked into her eyes and held her gaze without blinking.

"No," she said again. Her body relaxed. "We did the right thing. No regrets."

From the depths of the house, a bell chimed three times.

"That's us," she said.

They entered the passageway. The gray stone walls curved and descended deep below the house. They almost giggled at the torches lighting the way. Of course there were torches. It was as if such touches meant to calm them in an odd, reverse-psychology way.

It wasn't long before they entered a small anteroom. A couple they had met upstairs—now wearing only black, hooded cloaks—waited for them.

"Undress," the man said.

"Leave your clothes on the floor," the woman said.

Kind voices.

Janet and Merle removed their clothes and left them in a pile on the ground.

The cloaked couple pulled a black, velvet curtain aside and beckoned the McGees to enter.

The chamber was narrow but tall. A carved wooden likeness of a feminine goddess dominated the far wall. Two stone altars sat next to each other. The cloaked couple took their place with the other cloaked couples in a semi-circle around the altars. Mr. Melton stood at the front of the room, under the goddess image, wearing a red cloak.

Gentle hands guided Janet and Merle to the altars. They laid down on their backs. The altars were close enough for them to hold hands, which they did.

There were chants in strange languages. Candles were lit which gave off an intoxicating, dulling aroma. There were movements and dances which they could not see because they gazed only at each other. Janet saw the calm in Merle's eyes and the peace she found there flowed through her mind and spirit.

They had traded one year of unlimited luxury and comfort for this moment. The clink and tinkle of metal on metal sounded behind the chants. She glanced away long enough to see them taking long-bladed knives from a black velvet satchel. She smiled and looked back to Merle. Her thoughts returned to the old days, and even the fleeting memories filled her with sensations of bad odors and the taste of ashes in her mouth. Of unbearable worry and stress and terror of tomorrow. She turned away from that and returned to the peace for which they had paid so dearly.

The Wizard of Walnut Street

Jamie sat on the front step of the house where his family lived. The sun had set on his ninth Halloween. He watched as monsters, super-heroes, princesses, and other characters he didn't recognize passed by in pairs and groups. Parents followed, chatting and laughing and lighting the way with flashlights.

The maple tree in the front yard had shed its leaves. The brittle red leaves lined the edges of the sidewalk. A constant stream of trick--or-treaters crunched through them and kicked a fine dust into the air and filled the night with the aroma of the season. The grass had faded to light green, well on its way to a hibernating yellow. There was a slight breeze. The air was unseasonably warm. That meant no jacket required, so Jamie's King Arthur costume could be seen by the world. This much pleased him.

He finished the last two bites of his apple and sighed. The apple was a concession to his mother. At least eat something healthy, then enjoy the fruits of your Halloween labor. He often had to be cajoled into eat-ing something nutritious, but this apple was so fat and juicy and sweet it tasted like a fall day. Very satisfying.

So he had held up his end of the bargain, but the candy part of the evening was in doubt. His parents, after a pre-Halloween dinner at a burger joint, had both come down with a bug that socked them in what his father called "both ends." They were so sick that Dad passed out in bed. Mom apologized and mumbled something about calling Grandpa to come over before she also fell asleep. He knew his grandpa went to bed early. Jamie was likely on his own.

He doubted his parents would approve of him walking the streets alone. They might be okay if he joined another group, but they had fallen sick so fast that no details could be worked out. Maybe he could visit the neighbors on either side and across the street. He'd get a handful of sweets, but odds were good it would be at least twenty-five percent hard candy or Tootsie Rolls. What if he only got a single Snickers? Better than nothing, but torture considering what he had planned. At his age, it was feast or famine.

His plastic sword lay on the smooth concrete of the porch. He stared at it. It looked bored as did his empty candy sack. They needed adventure, the sword and sack, as did he.

Watching the other kids having fun was too much. He decided to go inside. King Arthur must keep for another year although he knew another character would catch his fancy by then. Choosing a costume was serious business. What a waste. On the bright side, *Frankenstein* was on TV tonight.

He stood up as a station wagon the size of a small tank navigated the holiday crowds and eased to a stop in front of the house. It took Jamie a second to recognize the car in the darkness, but before the driver got out, he knew who it was.

"Grandpa!"

"Hi, Skeezix!"

Karl Peddimore came around the station wagon with a slow, limping gait. Normally, he had a brisk stride for an eighty-year-old, but distant knee surgery had taken the spring out of his step. He leaned on an ebony cane with a silver handle. Jamie jumped to his feet and ran to greet his grandfather on the sidewalk. Karl playfully grunted as they hugged. Grandpa's clothes always smelled freshly cleaned, and the scent of Old Spice aftershave surrounded him.

"Everything okay here?" Karl asked. "Your mother called and sounded like her lips were taped shut."

God bless you, Mama. You made the call.

"They're sick," Jamie said. "They both had the chicken sandwich. I had the burger."

"Smart man."

"They got the Hershey squirts. Made 'em tired, I guess."

Karl nodded. "Having your ass go off like an oil rig will take it out of a person."

Jamie laughed.

"Don't tell your mother I said that."

"I won't."

"So who are you supposed to be? Let's see. Knight costume. Sword. Crown. You're Raggedy Ann?"

"Close, Grandpa."

"Hmm. King Arthur?"

"Yep!"

"Perfect. I'll feel safer walking the night with a great warrior."

"Can you walk okay?"

"Oh, I'll manage as long as you agree to pass along any butterscotch candies to me."

"Sure!"

He could have all the hard candy he wanted. Jamie wanted the *chocolate*.

"Speaking of Hershey's, let's get out there and get you some bounty!"

"Yeah!"

"Ah, I'd better leave your folks a note."

Karl went inside to scribble a note letting Jamie's parents know he was with his grandfather. Jamie bounced on the balls of his feet as he waited outside.

"Ready?" Jamie asked.

Karl chuckled. "One more delay. Sorry."

Jamie watched the other kids as Karl went to the rear of the station wagon. He wondered how long the neighborhood supply of Snickers and Twix would hold out.

"Open this ass-end door for me, would you?" Karl asked.

Jamie swung open the rear hatch.

"Gotta get my costume on," Karl said.

Jamie jumped with excitement. "You brought a costume?"

A black velvet bag yielded a long navy robe. Jamie helped Karl get it over his head. A long, conical hat completed the disguise. Glittering silver embroidery of sun, moon, and stars adorned both hat and robe.

"Wow!" Jamie said.

"You like it? Kids always did. I used to be a wizard, you know."

"For birthday parties and stuff?"

"Sure," Karl said. "Now I've kept you waiting long enough. Let's get that candy."

Jamie led them along as they went house to house.

"How many Halloweens have you had, Grandpa?" Jamie asked between houses.

"Hard to remember. All of 'em, I'd say."

"What did you dress up as for the first Halloween?"

"Same thing I wore when the wheel was invented," Karl said, gesturing to his outfit.

Jamie ducked away from the conversation to ring the next doorbell. He ran back with his hand out.

"Butterscotch!" Jamie said.

Karl's face lit up as he took the three gold discs and put one in his mouth. He turned toward the house and waved his silver-tipped cane.

"May growth and good health find this house," he said.

They walked on to the next house. Jamie didn't notice that the annual flowers lining the house's front, fading for the season, had sprung to colorful life again.

A trio of kids younger than Jamie—an angel, Batman, and a princess —ran past them screaming. Jamie shook his head.

"Everyone gets so crazy when it's Halloween."

He went to the door of the next house. Karl watched the three kids run away with a frown. Jamie returned.

"Pixie Stix. They're okay. You want 'em?"

"Goodness, no. If I put that much sugar in my old body I'd have a stroke."

Together they walked along the sidewalk. The porch lights of the next two houses are dark, so they continued on. Jamie noticed his grandpa walked at a faster pace, his limp gone, the cane swinging beside him. He said nothing.

"Houses along this block are dark every year," Jamie said. "Don't know why."

"They're close to the Brundom House, yes?"

"That creepy old place? Yeah. You think that's why?"

"I suppose the people who live there just don't like Halloween," Karl said. "Maybe they leave town."

"Maybe they hide under the bed," Jamie said with grin.

Karl turned to him with a grave look.

"I've kept an eye on the Brundom House for cent—, uh, I mean many years."

Jamie felt a chill. "Why?"

From up the street came screams and shouts. More kids ran toward them and past. Even grownups were on the run. Jamie looked up at his grandpa.

"What should we do?"

A tall man saw them as he ran past. "I don't know what it is, but you better run!"

Karl looked at Jamie.

"Should we go home and call the police?" the boy asked.

"Not much the police can do about what's happening up there."

"What's going on, Grandpa?"

"I knew this would happen. It's always been a possibility. Just when I thought it was done for good."

Jamie stared at him. "Are you really a wizard?"

"This morning I watched the leaves fall," Karl said. "It took them an unnatural length of time to find the ground. Even with the breeze, they stayed in the air too long. The field of gravity has been altered, but so slight as to be unnoticed at first. But I know. I've seen it happen before."

"Gravity?" Jamie asked, confused.

"Let's see one of the Pixie Stix."

Jamie dug one out of his bag and handed it over. Karl tore off the edge and dumped the contents into the air. Jamie watched wide-eyed as the sugary powder hovered in the air like a cloud before slowly—much slower than normal—settling onto the sidewalk.

"Whoa!"

"It's the little things, Skeezix."

An entire mob of parents and children ran away from an unknown terror up the street.

"You are heir to a line of guardians, Jamie. Guardians of time and space. I had hoped he wouldn't awaken until you were older, but sometimes we must have faith we'll be ready when we need to be."

"What does all of that mean?"

"It means when everyone runs away, we walk toward."

Karl walked forward, against the stream of humanity running in the opposite direction.

"You'll need your sword," Karl said.

Jamie held up his plastic sword, puzzled. "This?"

"Oh."

Karl tapped his cane against Jamie's sword. The plastic turned to metal, and with the sudden weight change the tip clanged to the pavement.

"You'll have to wield it better than that," Karl said with a wink.

Jamie stared at his new sword, mouth agape.

"It will be safer for both of us if you stop being surprised by everything," Karl said. "From now on expect anything."

"Right."

Jamie raised his sword in a two-hand grip. His face was grim and determined.

"That's the spirit," Karl said, patting his shoulder.

They came to the top of the hill where Brundom House dominated like a sinister mountain peak. The old, dark Victorian house was in disrepair, but still formidable. The streets and sidewalks around them were empty and deserted.

"The windows," Jamie said.

Red lights flickered though the dirty glass, chasing from one window to the other. The shingles and siding and framework shook from an interior quake.

"In we go," Karl said.

"What do I do?"

"Swing your sword when I tell you."

When Karl's foot touched the first step, the house went still. Karl looked at Jamie with a grin.

"We're old friends."

They ascended the steps, and the house shook again. Karl bellowed a phrase in an unknown language and swung his cane in a wide arc. Two things happened. The front door slammed open, and the cane stretched into a long staff. The flickering red lights became a pulse, powerful and hot.

Karl strode into the house showing no fear. Jamie was terrified, but followed.

The inside of the house was a funhouse of bizarre flaunting of physics. The grand staircase undulated as if it were a curtain flapping in the wind. The floorboards opened and closed over a red, smoky chasm like hungry teeth.

"Stay to the edge of the room, boy. Along the walls."

Another shouted incantation, and the house settled down. The boards knocked against their nails, trying to escape, but it was much quieter.

"Come forth," Karl said in a mocking voice. "You anticipated no fight."

The floorboards fell away, opening to a wide, jagged mouth filled with churning yellow and red molten stone.

"Looks like a volcano!" Jamie yelled, instantly feeling stupid for it.

"So you have awakened," Karl shouted.

A long, low moan rose from the void. Jamie readied his sword.

A disembodied voice spoke from below. The deep bass shook Jamie's bones and raised his hair. "*Old . . . you.*"

"Not so old as you."

"*You . . . this . . . time . . . lose.*"

"My powers have not waned."

"*Fight . . . we . . . now . . . must.*"

"Back to the void with you."

"*Not . . . before . . . must . . . eat.*"

Karl looked at Jamie. "The stakes are high, Sir Knight. Understand?"

Jamie nodded so fast he made himself dizzy.

The house went still as the chasm stirred with fury. First one, then two, then many tentacles reached up from the fiery abyss. Karl aimed his staff, shouted another undecipherable spell, and a bolt of jagged blue flame zapped a tentacle, severing it from the unseen beast. Jamie froze.

"Your sword, Sir Knight!," Karl cried. "Time to wield your sword!"

Jamie snapped out of his fear. He swung the heavy metal blade at the nearest tentacle. The slimy, quivering arm was wider than he. The sword bit three-quarters into the thick flesh. A second swing, along with a primal scream, cut it free.

Seven massive tentacles reached through the hole and swung about the house, destroying the stairs, smashing windows and breaking down walls. Together, Karl and Jamie fought the creature. A tentacle swatted Jamie hard to the floor. It quickly wrapped itself around his torso. Jamie chopped at the arm in a panic, but two deadly lightning strikes from Karl's staff freed the boy to fight on.

Despite his renewed energy when he donned his wizard outfit, Jamie knew Karl would tire out from the battle. He felt fatigue working through his own young, energetic body.

"*Won't . . . last . . . long.*"

Karl barely jumped away from a striking tentacle. Jamie saw the exhaustion and worry in his face. He wondered for the first time of they would survive.

Jamie steeled himself and removed another tentacle. It took four swings this time. The beast roared with rage. A surviving tentacle lashed out at Karl and knocked the staff away. A second arm struck like a snake and wrapped up the wizard, squeezing him tight.

"No!" Jamie screamed.

All was still as the beast raised Karl high into the air. The ground shook as the creature rose up from the void. An immense, bloodshot eye peeked over the shattered floorboards, staring at Jamie. For several seconds it didn't move, only stared.

Jamie looked up at his grandpa. He was exhausted. His arms pinned. Unable to move or draw breath for another spell.

The monster's jagged lips didn't move. It spoke through its malevolent mind.

"*You . . . go . . . inside.*"

The thing opened its awful mouth, revealing hideous gullet lined with teeth.

"*You . . . inside . . . he . . . live.*"

Karl angrily shook his head. Jamie, petrified, didn't move. The thing squeezed Karl. He let out a gasping cry of pain.

"Stop!" Jamie screamed.

It released it's grip, and Karl caught his breath.

"Sorry, Grandpa. I have to."

Jamie stepped forward. A malicious rumble of laughter shook the house anew. Jamie came closer. He could smell the awful breath of the thing. Karl struggled against the grip of the dripping tentacle. The monster laughed and laughed.

When the laughter was too loud to bear and the creature distracted, Jamie roared and plunged his sword into the huge, pulsating eye. He pushed it into the hilt and jogged back.

The thing dropped Karl and bellowed with pain and rage. Karl staggered to his feet and ran to his staff. Jamie ducked and dodged as the remaining tentacles slammed blindly around the house. He would be crushed in seconds if it found him.

Karl raised his staff, uttered another forbidden phrase, and a final bolt of blue lightning left his staff and found the grip of Jamie's sword. The metal blade conducted the energy deep into the creature's brain and throughout its body. Tentacles shot straight and rigid into the air.

Karl mercilessly pumped the lethal beam into his old enemy.

When the pulsating energy that lit up the eye was dark and empty, Karl released the beam.

In slow motion the beast fell back into the earth. The walls of the red and yellow void returned to their earthly color as it descended. Karl spoke his magic language again, and Jamie's sword pulled free from the eye. It hovered in mid-air as the monster fell.

The beast was gone. The house ravaged but standing.

Karl maneuvered the sword away from the void and dropped it on the floor. They regarded the gooey weapon with disgust.

"You'll want to rinse that off," Karl said.

By ten p.m., they were back at Karl's place. His wizard costume was back in its black velvet sack. He now wore his robe and slippers. Jamie had his candy sorted on the carpet, already working on the chocolate. He'd collected a fair amount of hard candy for his grandpa, who worked on that in-between bites of popcorn. They had missed *Frankenstein* thanks to their adventure, but the second feature, *Dracula*, had just started.

"That was awesome," Jamie said.

Karl chuckled. "Yes, I suppose it was."

"What was that thing?"

"A creature from another reality. I've battled him before. You'd need a second tongue to say its name properly, but for thousands of years, it's been known as Zig-Zil. We didn't kill it. Just gave it a good spanking. It'll be back, although it will be decades before it's powerful enough."

"Looked like a mutant squid."

Karl shrugged. "According to the lore of my order, the cephalopods —you know, octopus, squid, and so on—used to rule Earth in the long ago, ancient days. They are not of this world. These intelligences faded into other dimensions as time and matter changed and mankind grew dominant. But they desire to rule. They won't stop trying to come back."

"And you've fought them your whole life?"

"Our order rose up to defend man's sovereignty over Earth. We're not perfect custodians, by any means, but far more benevolent than they."

"Can I join?"

"I think you already have."

"Cool!"

They turned their attention to the television, hypnotized by Bela Lugosi's stare.

"Best not to tell your mother about tonight," Karl said.

They looked at each other, then laughed.

"She doesn't know you're a wizard?" Jamie asked.

"Membership in our order passes through our families. Your mother showed no interest nor aptitude. It skips generations sometimes."

Jamie sat on the sofa next to Karl, who put his arm around his grandson.

"Can we stay up and watch all the movies tonight?"

"Of course. Can't have an early bedtime on Halloween."

Jamie grinned. What a perfect night. On the carpet he saw a butterscotch disc that had escaped his notice. He was about to lean down and get it when he heard his grandpa snore.

Jamie settled back into the sofa. Grandpa's snore sounded like a chainsaw on metal, and Jamie swallowed a laugh. He lowered the volume on the television.

He thought about how life sometimes swerves gloriously away from the normal. When that happens you hope time stands still forever. The ebony cane, now returned to its normal shape and size, rested by the front door. Jamie studied it, memorizing its detail, along with everything else of the moment. His grandpa's sleeping arm rested heavily on his shoulder, and Jamie loved him very much.

About the Author

James B. Christensen is a novelist, screenwriter, musician, husband, and father of twin daughters. He is also the author of *"Honeymoon Phase,"* a supernatural romantic comedy, and *"The Vessel,"* an occult horror thriller. He lives in Omaha, Nebraska.

Visit jamesbchristensen.com to sign up for his monthly newsletter and stay informed of upcoming releases.